A PENGUIN MYSTERY

MY FRIEND MAIGRET

GEORGES JOSEPH CHRISTIAN SIMENON was born on February 12, 1903 in Liège, Belgium. He began work as a reporter for a local newspaper at the age of sixteen, and at nineteen he moved to Paris to embark on a career as a novelist. He started by writing pulp-fiction novels and novellas published, under various pseudonyms, from 1923 onwards. He went on to write seventy-five Maigret novels and twenty-eight Maigret short stories.

Although Simenon is best known in Britain as the writer of the Maigret books, his prolific output of over four hundred novels made him a household name and institution in Continental Europe, where much of his work is constantly in print. The dark realism of Simenon's books has lent them naturally to screen adaptation.

Simenon died in 1989 in Lausanne, Switzerland, where he had lived for the latter part of his life.

MY FRIEND MAIGRET

GEORGES SIMENON

MY FRIEND MAIGRET

TRANSLATED BY
NIGEL RYAN

PENGUIN BOOKS

PENGUIN BOOKS

Published by the Penguin Group

Penguin Group (USA) Inc., 375 Hudson Street, New York, New York 10014, U.S.A.
Penguin Group (Canada), 90 Eglinton Avenue East, Suite 700, Toronto,
Ontario, Canada M4P 2Y3 (a division of Pearson Penguin Canada Inc.)
Penguin Books Ltd, 80 Strand, London WC2R 0RL, England
Penguin Ireland, 25 St Stephen's Green, Dublin 2, Ireland (a division of Penguin Books Ltd)
Penguin Group (Australia), 250 Camberwell Road, Camberwell,
Victoria 3124, Australia (a division of Pearson Australia Group Pty Ltd)
Penguin Books India Pvt Ltd, 11 Community Centre,
Panchsheel Park, New Delhi – 110 017, India
Penguin Group (NZ), 67 Apollo Drive, Rosedale,
North Shore 0632, New Zealand (a division of Pearson New Zealand Ltd)
Penguin Books (South Africa) (Pty) Ltd, 24 Sturdee Avenue,
Rosebank, Johannesburg 2196, South Africa

Penguin Books Ltd, Registered Offices:
80 Strand, London WC2R 0RL, England

First published as *Mon ami Maigret* 1949
This translation first published by Hamish Hamilton 1956
Reissued, with minor revisions in Penguin Classics 2003
Published as a Penguin Red Classic 2006
This edition published by Penguin Books (USA) 2007

3 5 7 9 10 8 6 4

Copyright © 1949 by Georges Simenon Ltd (a Chorion company).
Translation copyright © 1956 by Georges Simenon Ltd
All rights reserved

LIBRARY OF CONGRESS CATALOGING IN PUBLICATION DATA
Simenon, Georges, 1903–1989.
[Mon ami Maigret. English]
My friend Maigret / Georges Simenon; translated by Nigel Ryan.
p. cm.—(A Penguin mystery)
ISBN 978-0-14-311284-6
1. Maigret, Jules (Fictitious character)—Fiction.
2. Porquerolles Island (France)—Fiction. I. Ryan, Nigel. II. Title.
PQ2637.I53M5713 2008
843'.912—dc22 2007025931

Printed in the United States of America

CONTENTS

CONTENTS

MY FRIEND MAIGRET

MY FRIEND MAIGRET

1

"You were standing in the doorway of your club?"

"Yes, officer."

It was no good remonstrating with him. Four or five times Maigret had tried to make him say "inspector." What did it matter anyway? What did all this matter?

"A gray sports car stopped for a moment and a man got out, with a flying leap almost, that's what you said, isn't it?"

"Yes, officer."

"To get into your club he must have passed close to you and even brushed against you. Now there's a luminous neon sign above the door."

"It's purple, officer."

"So what?"

"So nothing."

"Just because your sign is purple you are incapable of recognizing the individual who a moment later tore aside the velvet curtain and emptied his revolver into your barman?"

The man was called Caracci or Caraccini (Maigret was obliged to consult the dossier each time). He was short, but with high heels, a Corsican head (they still bear a faint resemblance to Napoleon), and he wore an enormous yellow diamond on his finger.

This had been going on since eight o'clock in the morning and it was now striking eleven. In actual fact it had been going on since the middle of the night, as all the people who had been rounded up in the Rue Fontaine, at the club where the barman had been shot down, had spent the night in the police station. Three or four detectives, including Janvier and Torrence, had already been working on Caracci, or Caraccini, without getting anything out of him.

It was May, but for all that the rain was falling as in the heaviest of autumn downpours. It had been raining like this since four or five o'clock, and the roofs, window ledges, and umbrellas made reflections similar to the water of the Seine, which the chief inspector could see by twisting his neck.

Mr. Pyke did not move. He remained seated on his chair, in a corner, as rigid as if he were in a waiting room, and it was beginning to be exasperating. His eyes travelled slowly from the chief inspector to the little man and from the little man to the chief inspector, without it being possible to guess what was going on in his English official's mind.

"You realize, Caracci, that your attitude could cost you dear, and that your club might well be closed down for good and all?"

The Corsican, unimpressed, gave Maigret a conspiratorial wink, smiled, smoothed the ends of his black mustache with his ringed finger.

"I've always gone straight, officer. Try asking your colleague, Priollet."

Although there was a corpse, it was actually Chief Inspector Priollet, chief of the Vice Squad, that the case concerned, owing to the particular circumstances in which it had all started. Unfortunately Priollet was in the Jura at the funeral of some relation.

"In short, you refuse to speak?"

"I don't refuse, officer."

Maigret, heavily, looking disgruntled, went and opened the door.

"Lucas! Work on him a bit longer."

Oh, the way Mr. Pyke stared at him! Mr. Pyke might be the nicest man on earth, but there were moments when Maigret caught himself hating him. Exactly the same as with his brother-in-law, who was called Mouthon. Once a year in the spring, Mouthon got off the train at the Gare de l'Est with his wife, who was Madame Maigret's sister.

He, too, was the nicest man on earth; he would never have hurt a fly. As for his wife, she was gaiety personified, and from the moment she arrived in the flat in the Boulevard Richard-Lenoir, she would call for an apron to help with the housework. On the first day it was perfect. The second day, it was almost as perfect.

"We're leaving tomorrow," Mouthon would then announce.

"I won't hear of it!" Madame Maigret would protest. "Why leave so soon?"

"Because we'll be getting in your way."

"Not on your life!"

Maigret would also declare with conviction:

"Not on your life!"

On the third day, he would hope that some unexpected job would prevent his dining at home. Now never, since his sister-in-law had married Mouthon and the couple had been coming to see them every year, never, ever, had one of those cases which keep you out of doors for days and nights on end cropped up at that moment.

From the fifth day onwards his wife and he would exchange agonized glances, and the Mouthons would stay for nine days, invariably pleasant, charming, thoughtful, as discreet as could be, so that one felt more guilty than ever for coming to detest them.

It was the same with Mr. Pyke. However, it was now only three days that he had been accompanying Maigret wherever he went. One day, during the holidays, they had said to Mouthon, idly:

"Why not come and spend a week in Paris, in the spring? We have a guest room which is always empty."

They had come.

Similarly, a few weeks back, the Chief of Police had paid an official visit to the Lord Mayor of London. The latter had had him shown round the offices of the famous Scotland Yard, and the chief had been agreeably surprised to discover that the senior officers of the English police knew Maigret by repute and were interested in his methods.

"Why don't you come and see him at work?" the worthy man had said.

They had taken him at his word. Just like the Mouthons. They had sent over Inspector Pyke, and for the last three days the latter had followed Maigret about everywhere, as discreet, as self-effacing as could be. He was nonetheless there.

In spite of his thirty-five or forty years he looked so young that he reminded one of a serious-minded student. He was certainly intelligent, perhaps even acutely so. He looked, listened, reflected. He reflected so much that one seemed to be able to hear him reflecting, and it was beginning to be wearing.

It was a little as though Maigret had been placed under observation. All his acts, all his words were carefully sifted in the cranium of the impassive Mr. Pyke.

For three days now there had been nothing interesting to do. Just routine. Red tape. Uninteresting interrogations, like the one with Caracci.

They had come to understand one another, Pyke and he, without anything being said. For example, the moment the nightclub owner had been led off to the sergeants' room, where the door had been carefully closed, there was no mistaking the question in the Englishman's eyes:

"Rough stuff?"

Probably, yes. You don't put on velvet gloves to deal with people like Caracci. So what? It was of no importance. The case was without interest. If the barman had been done in it was probably because he hadn't been playing straight, or because he had belonged to a rival gang. Periodically, these characters settle their accounts, kill one another off, and in the long run, it is a good riddance.

Whether Caracci talked or held his peace, there would sooner or later be someone who would take the bait, very likely a police informer. Did they have informers in England?

"Hallo! . . . Yes . . . It's me . . . Who? . . . Lechat? . . . Don't know him . . . Where do you say he's calling from? . . . Porquerolles? Put him through . . ."

The Englishman's eye was still riveted upon him like the eye of God in the story of Cain.

"Hallo! . . . I can't hear very well . . . Lechat? . . . Yes . . . Right . . . I got that . . . Porquerolles . . . I got that too . . ."

With the receiver to his ear he was looking at the rain which was streaming down the windowpanes and thinking that there must be sunshine at Porquerolles, a small island in the Mediterranean off Hyères and Toulon. He had never been there, but he had often been told about it. People came back from it as brown as Bedouins. In fact it was the first time anyone had telephoned him from an island and he told himself that the telephone wires must pass under the sea.

"Yes . . . What? . . . A short fair-haired fellow, at Luçon? . . . Ah yes, I remember . . ."

He had met an Inspector Lechat when, as a result of some rather complicated administrative postings, he had been sent for a few months to Luçon, in the Vendée.

"You're at present with the flying squad at Draguignan, right. And you're ringing from Porquerolles . . ."

There was a crackling noise on the line. Every now and then the girls could be heard interrupting from one town to another.

"Hallo! Paris . . . Paris . . . Hallo! Paris . . . Paris. . ."

"Hallo! Toulon . . . Are you Toulon, dearie? Hallo! Toulon . . ."

Did the telephone work better on the other side of the channel? Impassive, Mr. Pyke listened and looked at him, and for appearances' sake Maigret toyed with a pencil.

"Hallo! . . . Do I know a Marcellin? . . . What Marcellin? . . . What? . . . A fisherman? . . . Try to make yourself clear, Lechat . . . I can't understand what you're talking about . . . A character who lives in a boat . . . Right . . . Go on . . . He claims to be a friend of mine? . . . What? . . . He used to claim? . . . He's dead? . . . He was killed last night? . . . That's nothing to do with me, Lechat, old man . . . It's not my area . . . He had talked about me all evening? . . . And you say that is why he's dead? . . ."

He had dropped his pencil and was trying, with his free hand, to relight his pipe.

"I'm making a note, yes . . . Marcel . . . It's not Marcellin anymore . . . As you say . . . *P* for Paul . . . *A* for Arthur . . . *C* for cinema . . . yes . . . Pacaud . . . You've sent off fingerprints? . . . A letter from me? . . . Are you sure? . . . Headed paper? . . . What heading? . . . Brasserie des Ternes. It's possible . . . And what did I say? . . ."

If only Mr. Pyke hadn't been there and hadn't been looking at him so earnestly!

"I'm writing it down, yes . . . 'Ginette leaves tomorrow for the sanatorium. She sends her love. Sincerely . . .' It's signed Maigret? . . . No, it's not necessarily a forgery . . . I seem to remember something . . . I'll go and look in the files . . . Go down there? . . . You know perfectly well it's no business of mine . . ."

He was just going to hang up, but he couldn't resist asking one question, at the risk of shocking Mr. Pyke.

"Is the sun shining down there? . . . Mistral? . . . But there's sun as well? . . . Okay . . . If I've any news I'll call you back . . . I promise . . ."

If Mr. Pyke asked few questions, he had a way of looking at you that obliged Maigret to speak.

"You know the island of Porquerolles?" he said, lighting his pipe. "It's supposed to be very beautiful, as beautiful as Capri and the Greek islands. A man was killed there last night, but it's not in my district. They found a letter from me in his boat."

"It really was from you?"

"Quite likely. The name Ginette seems to ring a bell. Are you coming upstairs with me?"

Mr. Pyke already knew all the departments of Police Headquarters, which he had been shown round. One behind the other they walked up to the attics, where files are kept on everyone who has had dealings with the police. On account of the Englishman, Maigret was suffering from a sort of inferiority complex, and he was ashamed of the antiquated clerk in long gray overalls, who was sucking cough drops.

"Tell me, Langlois . . . By the way, is the wife better?"

"It's not the wife, Monsieur Maigret. It's my mother-in-law."

"Oh yes! Sorry. Has she had her operation?"

"She went back home yesterday."

"Would you have a look and see if you've got anything under the name Marcel Pacaud? With a *d* at the end."

Was it any better in London? You could hear the rain hammering on the roof, cascading into the gutters.

"Marcel?" asked the clerk, perched on a ladder.

"That's right. Pass me his file."

Besides fingerprints, it contained a photograph, full face, and a profile, without collar or tie, under the crude light of the identity department.

"Pacaud, Marcel-Joseph-Étienne, born in Le Havre, seaman . . ."

Frowning, Maigret tried to remember, his eyes fixed on the photographs. The man, at the time they had been taken, was thirty-five. He was thin, sickly looking. A black bruise below the right eye seemed to indicate that he had been interrogated thoroughly before being handed over to the photographer.

There followed a long list of convictions. At Le Havre, aged seventeen, assault and battery. At Bordeaux, a year later, assault and battery again, with drunkenness on the public way. Resisted arrest. Assault and battery again in a house of ill repute in Marseilles.

Maigret held the file so as to let his English colleague read at the same time as himself, and Mr. Pyke showed no surprise, seemed to say:

"We have that over on the other side as well."

"Living on immoral earnings . . ."

Did they have that too? That meant Marcel Pacaud had been a pimp. And, in the usual way, he had been sent off to do his military service in the Africa Battalions.

"Assault and battery, at Nantes . . ."

"Assault and battery, at Toulon . . ."

"A thug," Maigret said simply to Mr. Pyke.

Then it became more serious.

"Paris. Inveigling."

The Englishman asked:

"What's that?"

Imagine having to explain that to a man who belongs to a race with the reputation of being the most tight-laced in the world!

"It's a sort of theft, but a theft committed in special circumstances. When a gentleman accompanies an unknown lady to a more or less disreputable hotel and then goes and complains that his wallet has been stolen, it's called inveigling. Nearly always the prostitute has an accomplice. You follow me?"

"I understand."

There were three convictions for acting as accomplice to inveigling on Marcel Pacaud's file, and on each occasion, there was a certain Ginette in the case.

Then things became worse still, for there was an incident involving a knife wound which Pacaud was supposed to have inflicted on a recalcitrant gentleman.

"They're what you call *mauvais garçons*, I believe?" Mr. Pyke insinuated gently; his French was terribly impregnated with nuances, so much so that it became ironical.

"Precisely. I wrote to him, I recall. I don't know how you deal with them in your country."

"Very correctly."

"I don't doubt it. Here we sometimes knock them around. We're not always gentle with them. But the odd thing is that they seldom hold it against us. They know we're only doing our job. From one interrogation to the next, we get to know each other."

"This is the one who called himself a friend of yours?"

"I'm convinced he was sincere. I particularly remember the girl and what I remember still better is the headed paper. If we have the chance I'll show you the Brasserie des Ternes. It's very comfortable and the sauerkraut is excellent. Do you like sauerkraut?"

"On occasion," replied the Englishman, without enthusiasm.

"Every afternoon and evening there are a few women sitting round a table. It's there that Ginette used to work. A Breton girl, who came from a village in the St. Malo area. She started off as a maid of all work with a local butcher. She adored Pacaud, and when he talked of her, tears would come into his eyes. Does that surprise you?"

Nothing surprised Mr. Pyke, whose expression betrayed no emotion whatsoever.

"I became rather interested in them, at one time. She was riddled with TB. She hadn't wanted to have herself cured because that would have taken her away from her Marcel. When he was in prison, I persuaded her to go to see one of my friends, a specialist on consumption, and he got her into a sanatorium in Savoie. That's all."

"That's what you wrote to Pacaud?"

"That's right. Pacaud was at Fresnes and I hadn't time to go there myself."

Maigret gave the file back to Langlois and started down the stairs.

"How about going to eat?"

This was another problem, almost a case for his conscience. If he took Mr. Pyke for his meals into too luxurious restaurants he risked giving his colleagues from across the channel the impression that the French police spend most of their time junketing. If, on the other hand, he took him to places where only set meals are served, perhaps they would accuse him of stinginess.

Same with apéritifs. To drink them or not to drink them?

"Are you expecting to go to Porquerolles?"

Did Mr. Pyke want to make a trip to the Midi?

"It's not up to me to decide. In theory I don't operate outside Paris and the department of the Seine."

The sky was gray, a lowering, hopeless gray, and even the word "mistral" took on a tempting allure.

"Do you like tripe?"

He took him to the Market, and made him eat *tripes à la mode de Caen* and crêpes Suzette, which were brought to them on attractive copper chafing dishes.

"This is what we call an empty sort of day."

"So do we."

What could the Scotland Yard man be thinking of him? He had come to study "Maigret's methods" and Maigret had no method. He found only a large, rather clumsy man who must appear to him to be the prototype of the French public servant. How long would he go on following him about like that?

At two o'clock they were back at the Quai des Orfèvres, and Caracci was still there, in the kind of glass cage that served as a waiting room. That meant they had got nothing out of him and they were going to question him again.

"Has he eaten?" Mr. Pyke asked.

"I don't know. Possibly. Sometimes they have a sandwich brought up for them."

"And otherwise?"

"They let them fast a little to prompt the memory."

"The chief is asking for you, inspector."

"Will you excuse me, Mr. Pyke?"

That was something to the good. The other wouldn't follow him into the chief's office.

"Come in, Maigret. I've just had a call from Draguignan."

"I know what that's about."

"Lechat has of course been in touch with you. Have you much work at the moment?"

"Not too much. Apart from my guest . . ."

"Does he get in your way?"

"He's the soul of discretion."

"Do you remember the man called Pacaud?"

"I remembered him when I looked up his file."

"Don't you find the story rather odd?"

"I only know what Lechat told me on the telephone and he was so eager to explain that I didn't understand very much."

"The commissioner talked to me at great length. He insists on your going for a trip down there. According to him it's because of you that Pacaud was killed."

"Because of me?"

"He can't see any other explanation for the murder. For several years Pacaud, better known under the name of Marcellin, had lived at Porquerolles in his boat. He had become a popular figure. As far as I could gather he was more like a tramp than a fisherman. In the winter he lived without doing anything. In the summer he took tourists out fishing round the islands. No one had anything to gain by his death. He wasn't known to have had enemies. Nothing was stolen from him, for the very good reason that there was nothing to steal."

"How was he killed?"

"That's just what intrigues the commissioner."

The chief consulted several notes which he had made during his telephone conversation.

"As I don't know the place, it's difficult for me to get an accurate picture. The evening before last . . ."

"I thought I was told it was yesterday . . ."

"No, the day before. A number of people were gathered at the Arche de Noé. That must be an inn or a café. At this time of year, it seems, only the habitués are to be seen there. Everyone knows everyone else. Marcellin was there. In the course of an almost general conversation he mentioned you."

"Why?"

"I've no idea. People talk freely about celebrities. Marcellin claimed you were a friend of his. Perhaps some people had cast doubts on your professional abilities. The fact remains that he defended you with uncommon vigor."

"Was he drunk?"

"He was always more or less drunk. There was a strong mistral blowing. I don't know what effect the mistral has down there, but as far as I can gather, it is of some importance. It was chiefly on account of this mistral that Marcellin, instead of sleeping in his boat, as he normally did, went off in the direction of a hut which stands near the harbor, where the fishermen spread out their nets. When he was found, the next morning, he had received several shots in the head, fired at point-blank range, and one in the shoulder. The murderer emptied his gun on him. Not content with that he hit him in the face with a heavy instrument. It seems he put an extraordinary ferocity into it."

Maigret looked at the Seine, outside, through the curtain of rain, and thought of the Mediterranean sun.

"Boisvert, the commissioner, is a pleasant fellow, whom I've known for ages. He doesn't usually get carried away. He's just arrived on the scene, but he has to leave again this evening. He agrees with Lechat in thinking it was the conversation about you which started the thing off. He's not far from saying that it was you, in a sort of way, that was being aimed at through Marcellin. See what I mean? A man who has a big enough grudge against you to go for anyone who claims to be a friend of yours and sticks up for you."

"Are there people like that at Porquerolles?"

"That's what's puzzling Boisvert. On an island everyone is known. No one can land and go off again

without it being known. So far there isn't the remotest
suspect. Or else they'll have to suspect people without
any grounds. What do you think?"

"I think Mr. Pyke would like a trip to the Midi."

"And you?"

"I think I'd like it too if it was a question of going by
myself."

"When will you be leaving?"

"I'll take the night train."

"With Mr. Pyke?"

"With Mr. Pyke!"

Did the Englishman imagine the French police had
powerful motorcars at their disposal to take them to the
scenes of crimes?

He must think, at any rate, that Police Headquarters
detectives have unlimited expenses for their movements.
Had Maigret done right? Alone, he would have been content with a couchette. At the Gare de Lyon he hesitated.
Then at the last moment he took two wagon-lit places.

It was sumptuous. In the corridor they found de luxe
travelers, with impressive-looking luggage. An elegant
crowd, laden with flowers, was seeing a film star on to
the train.

"It's the Blue Train," Maigret mumbled, as if to
excuse himself.

If only he had been able to know what his fellow
policeman was thinking! Into the bargain they were

obliged to undress in front of one another and, the next morning, they would have to share the minute washing compartment.

"Well," said Mr. Pyke, in dressing gown and pajamas, "so a case is under way."

Just what did he mean by that? His French had something so precise about it that he always looked for a hidden meaning.

"It's a case, yes."

"Did you take a copy of Marcellin's file?"

"No. I confess I never thought of it."

"Have you concerned yourself at all about what has become of the woman: Ginette, I believe?"

"No."

Was there a reproach in the look Mr. Pyke shot at him?

"Have you brought an open arrest warrant with you?"

"Not that either. Only an interrogation permit, which entitles me to summon people and question them."

"Do you know Porquerolles?"

"I've never set foot there. I hardly know the Midi. I was on a case there, once, at Antibes and Cannes, and I remember particularly it was overpoweringly hot and I felt permanently sleepy."

"Don't you like the Mediterranean?"

"In general, I dislike places where I lose the desire to work."

"That's because you like working, is it?"

"I don't know."

It was true. On the one hand he railed every time a case came along to interrupt his daily routine. On the other hand as soon as he was left in peace for several days he would become restless, as though anxious.

"Do you sleep well on trains?"

"I sleep well anywhere."

"The train doesn't help you think?"

"I think so little, you know!"

It embarrassed him to see the compartment filled with smoke from his pipe, the more so as the Englishman didn't smoke.

"So you don't know what line you are going to start on?"

"Quite right. I don't even know if there is a line."

"Thank you."

One could feel that Mr. Pyke had registered Maigret's every word, had carefully arranged them in order in his brain, for use later on. It could not have been more off-putting. One could imagine him, on his return to Scotland Yard, gathering his colleagues round him (why not in front of a blackboard?) and announcing in his precise voice:

"A case conducted by Chief Inspector Maigret . . ."

And what if it was a flop? If it was one of those stories where one flounders about and only finds out the solution ten years later, by the merest fluke? If it was a humdrum affair, if tomorrow Lechat rushed up to the carriage door, announcing:

"All over! We've arrested the drunkard who did it. He's confessed."

What if . . . Madame Maigret hadn't put a dressing gown in his suitcase. She hadn't wanted him to take the old one, which looked like a monk's habit, and he had been meaning to buy a new one for the last two months. He felt indecent in his nightshirt.

"How about a nightcap?" suggested Mr. Pyke, offering him a silver whisky flask and cup. "That's what we call the last whisky before going to bed."

He drank a cupful of whisky. He didn't like it. Perhaps, equally, Mr. Pyke didn't like the calvados that Maigret had been making him take for the last three days.

He slept and was conscious of snoring. When he woke, he saw olive trees on the edge of the Rhône and knew they had passed Avignon.

The sun was shining, a light golden mist above the river. The Englishman, freshly shaved, immaculate from head to foot, was standing in the corridor, his face pressed to the window. The washing compartment was as clean as if he had never used it and there lurked a discreet smell of lavender.

Not yet sure if he was in a good temper or a bad one Maigret grumbled as he fumbled in his suitcase for his razor:

"Now we must be careful not to make a balls of this."

Perhaps it was the impeccable correctness of Mr. Pyke that made him coarse . . .

2

And so the first round had been fairly successfully concluded. Which does not mean that there had been any competition between the two men, at least not on professional grounds. If Mr. Pyke was more or less participating in Maigret's activities as a policeman, it was purely in the role of spectator.

Yet Maigret was thinking in terms of "first round," aware that it was not quite accurate. Hasn't one the right to use one's own private language, in one's own mind?

When he had joined the English detective in the Pullman corridor, for example, there was no doubt that the latter, taken by surprise, had not had time to efface the expression of wonder which quite transfigured him. Was it simply shame, because a Scotland Yard official is not supposed to give his attention to the sunrise on one of the most beautiful landscapes in the world? Or was the Englishman reluctant to show outward signs of admiration, considering it indecent in the presence of an alien witness?

Maigret had inwardly chalked up a point to himself, without a moment's hesitation.

In the restaurant car, he had to admit, Mr. Pyke had scored one in his turn. A mere nothing. A slight contraction of the nostrils on the arrival of the bacon and eggs, which were indisputably not so good as in his country.

"You don't know the Mediterranean, Mr. Pyke?"

"I usually spend my holidays in Sussex. I once went to Egypt though. The sea was gray and choppy, and it rained all the way."

And Maigret, who in his heart of hearts didn't like the Midi very much, felt himself spurred by the desire to defend it.

A questionable point: the headwaiter, who had recognized the chief inspector, whom he must have served elsewhere, came up and asked, in an insinuating voice, immediately after his breakfast:

"Something to drink, as usual?"

Now the day before, or the day before that, the Yard inspector had commented, with the air of one who never touches it, that an English gentleman never had strong drinks before the end of the afternoon.

The arrival at Hyères was without question a round in Maigret's favor. The palm trees, round the station, were motionless, transfixed in a Sahara sun. It was very likely that there had been an important market that morning, a fair or a fête, for the carts, vans, and heavy trucks were mobile pyramids of early vegetables, fruits, and flowers.

Mr. Pyke, just like Maigret, found his breath coming a little more quickly. There was a real sense of entering another world, and it was uncomfortable to do so in the dark clothes which had suited the previous day in the rainy streets of Paris.

He ought, like Inspector Lechat, to have worn a light suit and a shirt with an open collar, and shown a red patch of sunburn on his forehead. Maigret had not immediately recognized him, for he remembered his name rather than his face. Lechat, who was threading his way through the porters, looked almost like a boy from the district, small and thin, hatless, with espadrilles on his feet.

"This way, chief!"

Was this a good mark? For though this devil Mr. Pyke noted everything down, it was impossible to tell what he classified in the good column and what he put into the bad one. Officially Lechat ought to have called Maigret "chief inspector," for he was not in his department. But there were few detectives in France who could deny themselves the pleasure of calling him "chief" with affectionate familiarity.

"Mr. Pyke, you already know about Inspector Lechat. Lechat, let me introduce Mr. Pyke, from Scotland Yard."

"Are they in on it too?"

Lechat was so taken up with his Marcellin case that it didn't surprise him at all that it should have become an international affair.

"Mr. Pyke is in France on a study tour."

While they walked through the crowd Maigret wondered at the curious way Lechat was walking sideways, twisting his neck around.

"Let's hurry through," he was saying. "I've got a car at the entrance."

It was the small official car. Once inside the inspector heaved a sigh:

"I thought you'd better be careful. Everyone knows it's you *they've got it in for.*"

So just now, in the crowd, it was Maigret the tiny Lechat was trying to protect!

"Shall I take you straight to the island? You haven't anything to do in Hyères, have you?"

And off they went. The land was flat, deserted, the road lined with tamarisks, with a palm tree here and there, then white salt marshes on the right. The change of scene was as absolute as if they had been transported to Africa—with a blue porcelain sky, and the air perfectly still.

"And the mistral?" Maigret asked, with a touch of irony.

"It stopped quite suddenly yesterday evening. It was high time. It's blown for nine days and that's enough to drive everyone mad."

Maigret was skeptical. The people from the north—and the north begins around Lyon—have never taken the mistral seriously. So Mr. Pyke was excused for displaying indifference as well.

"No one has left the island. You can question everyone who was there when Marcellin was murdered. The
fishermen were not at sea that night because of the
storm. But a torpedo boat from Toulon and several sub-
marines were doing exercises in the lee of the island. I
rang up the Admiralty. They are positive. No boat
made the crossing."

"Which means the murderer is still on the island?"

"You'll see."

Lechat was playing the old boy, who knows his way
around and the people. Maigret was the new boy, which
is always rather a distasteful role. The car, after half an
hour, was slowing to a halt at a rocky promontory on
which there was nothing to be seen except a typical
Provençal inn and several fishermen's cottages painted
pink and pale blue.

One mark for France, for the mouth fell open. The sea
was an incredible blue, such as one normally only sees on
picture postcards, and over on the horizon an island
stretched lazily in the middle of the rainbowlike surface,
with bright green hills, and red and yellow rocks.

At the end of the wooden landing stage, a fishing boat
was waiting, painted pale green picked out in white.

"That's for us. I asked Gabriel to bring me over and
wait for you. The boat which does the regular service,
the *Cormorant*, only comes at eight in the morning and
five in the evening. Gabriel is a Galli. Let me explain.
There are Gallis and Morins. Almost everyone on the island belongs to one of the two families."

Lechat was carrying the luggage, which seemed to grow larger at the end of his arms. The engine was already turning over. It was all a little unreal and it was hard to believe that they were there solely to concern themselves with a dead man.

"I didn't suggest showing you the body. It's at Hyères. The postmortem took place yesterday morning."

There were about three miles between Giens Point and Porquerolles. As they advanced over the silky water the contours of the island became more distinct, with its peaks, its bays, its ancient fortresses in the greenery and, right in the middle, a small group of light-colored houses and the white church tower which might have come from a child's building set.

"Do you think I might be able to get hold of a bathing costume?" the Englishman asked Lechat.

Maigret hadn't thought of that and, leaning over the rail, he suddenly discovered, with a sense of vertigo, the bottom of the sea, which was slipping away under the boat. It was a good thirty feet below, but the water was so clear that the minutest details of the underwater landscape were visible. And it really was a landscape, with its plains covered in greenery, its rocky hills, its gorges and precipices, among which shoals of fish trooped like sheep.

A little put out, as though he had been surprised playing a child's game, Maigret looked at Mr. Pyke, but only to score another point: the Scotland Yard inspector, almost as moved as himself, was also gazing at the bottom of the water.

It is only after a while that one begins to take in the atmosphere of a place. At first everything seemed strange. The harbor was tiny, with a jetty on the left, a rocky promontory, covered with sea pines, on the right. In the background some red roofs, white and pink houses among the palm trees, the mimosas and the tamarisks.

Had Maigret ever seen mimosas before outside the flower girls' baskets in Paris? He couldn't remember whether the mimosas had been in flower at the time of the case he had conducted in Antibes and Cannes, a few years before.

On the jetty a handful of people were waiting. There were also some fishermen in boats painted like Christmas decorations.

They were watched as they disembarked. Perhaps the people on the island consisted of various groups? Maigret needn't bother about these details until later. For example, a man dressed in white, with a white cap on his head, greeted him with a hand to his forelock, and he didn't recognize him at first.

"That's Charlot!" Lechat whispered in his ear.

The name, for the moment, conveyed nothing to him. A sort of colossus with bare feet piled the luggage onto a barrow without uttering a word, and pushed it in the direction of the village square.

Maigret, Pyke, and Lechat followed. And behind them the locals followed in turn; all this in an odd silence.

The square was vast and deserted, enclosed by eucalyptus trees and colored houses, with, to crown it, the little yellow church and its white tower. They could see several cafés with shaded terraces.

"I could have booked you rooms at the Grand Hôtel. It has been open for a fortnight."

It was a fair-sized block overlooking the harbor, and a man dressed like a cook stood in the doorway.

"I thought it better to put you into the Arche de Noé. Let me explain."

There were already a lot of things for the inspector to explain. The terrace of the Arche, on the square, was wider than the others and was bounded by a small wall and green plants. Inside it was cool, a little dark, which was in no way disagreeable, and one was at once struck by the pronounced smell of cooking and of white wine.

Yet another man dressed as a cook, but without the chef's cap. He advanced with outstretched hand, a radiant smile on his face.

"Delighted to welcome you, Monsieur Maigret. I have given you the best room. Of course you will have a glass of our local white wine?"

Lechat whispered:

"That's Paul, the proprietor."

There were red tiles on the floor. The bar was a proper bistro bar, made of metal. The white wine was cool, a little young, but a good strong one.

"Your health, Monsieur Maigret. I never dared to hope that I should one day have the honor of having you to stay."

It didn't occur to him that it was to a crime that he owed the honor. No one seemed to bother about Marcellin's death. The groups they had just seen near the jetty were now in the square and imperceptibly approaching the Arche de Noé. Some of them were even sitting down on the terrace.

In short, what really mattered was Maigret's arrival, in flesh and blood, just as if he had been a film star.

Was he cutting a good figure? Did the Scotland Yard people have more self-assurance at the beginning of an investigation? Mr. Pyke looked at everything and said nothing.

"I should like to go and clean up a bit," Maigret sighed after a while, having drunk two glasses of white wine.

"Jojo! Will you show Monsieur Maigret up to his room? Will your friend be going up too, inspector?"

Jojo was a small dark servant girl, dressed in black, with a broad smile and small pointed breasts.

The whole house smelt of bouillabaisse and saffron oil. Upstairs, where there was red flooring as in the bar, there were only three or four rooms and they had in fact reserved the best for the chief inspector, the one with one window looking on to the square and the other on to the sea. Ought he to offer it to Mr. Pyke? It was too late. They had already indicated another door for the latter.

"Is there anything you want, Monsieur Maigret? The bathroom is at the end of the corridor. I think there's some hot water."

Lechat had followed him up. It was natural. It was normal. But he didn't ask him in. It seemed to him that it would be a sort of discourtesy toward his English colleague. The latter might imagine they were hiding something from him, that they weren't letting him in on the *whole* case.

"I'll be down in a few minutes, Lechat."

He would have liked to find a kindly word for the inspector, who was looking after him with such care. He seemed to recall that at Luçon his wife had come into the picture a lot. Standing in the doorway, he asked, in a friendly and familiar manner:

"How is your charming Madame Lechat?"

And the poor fellow could only stammer:

"Didn't you know? She left me. It's eight years ago now since she left."

What a gaffe! It all came back to him suddenly. If people talked so much about Madame Lechat at Luçon, it was because she deceived her husband for all she was worth.

In his bedroom he did nothing except take off his coat, wash his hands, teeth, and face, stretch in front of the window and lie on his bed for a few minutes as if to try out the springs. The furnishing was antiquated, agreeable, with always the good smell of southern cooking which pervaded every corner of the house. He hesitated about whether to go down in shirtsleeves, for it was hot, but decided that it would look too much like a holiday and put on his coat again.

When he arrived downstairs there were several people at the bar, mostly men in fishermen's clothes. Lechat was waiting for him in the doorway.

"Would you like a stroll, chief?"

"We'd better wait for Mr. Pyke."

"He's already gone out."

"Where?"

"Into the water. Paul lent him a bathing suit."

They headed unconsciously for the harbor. The slope of the ground led them there of its own accord. One felt that everyone was bound inevitably to take the same path.

"I think you'd better be very careful, chief. Whoever killed Marcellin has a grudge against you and will try to get you."

"We'd better wait until Mr. Pyke is out of the water."

Lechat pointed to a head which emerged on the far side of the boats.

"Is he on the case?"

"He's following it. We mustn't give the impression of plotting behind his back."

"We would have been quieter at the Grand Hôtel. It's closed in the winter. It has only just opened and there's no one there. Only it's at Paul's that everyone meets. It's there that it all began, because it was there that Marcellin mentioned you and claimed you were a friend of his."

"Let's wait for Mr. Pyke."

"Do you want to question people in his presence?"

"I shall have to."

Lechat made a wry face, but did not dare to protest.

"Where are you thinking of summoning them? There's hardly anywhere except the town hall. A single room with benches, a table, flags for July 14 and a bust of the Republic. The mayor keeps the grocer's shop, next to the Arche de Noé. That's him you can see over there, pushing a wheelbarrow."

Mr. Pyke was now coming back into his depth once more near a boat attached to a chain, was treading water, peacefully splashing in the sun.

"The water's marvelous," he said.

"If you like, we'll wait here while you go and get dressed."

"I'm very comfortable as I am."

This time it was a point to him. He was in fact just as much at his ease in bathing trunks, with drops of salt water trickling down his long, thin body, as in his gray suit.

He pointed to a black yacht, not in the harbor, but at anchor, several cables out. The English flag was discernible.

"Who's that?"

Lechat explained:

"The boat is called the *North Star*. It comes here almost every year. It belongs to a Mrs. Ellen Wilcox: that's also the name of a whisky, I believe. She's the owner of Wilcox whisky."

"Is she young?"

"She's fairly well preserved. She lives on board with her secretary, Philippe de Moricourt, and a crew of two. There's another Englishman on the island, who lives here all the year round. You can see his house from here. It's the one with the minaret beside it."

Mr. Pyke didn't look particularly enthusiastic at coming across fellow countrymen.

"It's Major Bellam, but the locals simply call him the major, and sometimes Teddy."

"I suppose he's an Indian Army major?"

"I don't know."

"Does he drink a lot?"

"Yes, a lot. You'll see him tonight at the Arche. You'll see everyone at the Arche, including Mrs. Wilcox and her secretary."

"Were they present when Marcellin spoke?" asked Maigret, for the sake of something to say, for in actual fact he was no longer interested in anything.

"They were. Practically everyone was at the Arche, as they are every evening. In a week or two the tourists begin to pour in and life will be different. For the moment it's not entirely the life of the winter, when the inhabitants are alone on the island, and it's not quite what is called the season. Only the regulars have arrived. I don't know if you follow me. Most of them have been coming here for years, and know everybody. The major has been living at the Minaret for eight years. The villa next to it belongs to Monsieur Émile."

Lechat looked at Maigret with a hesitant air. Perhaps, in the presence of the Englishman, he, too, was overcome with a sort of patriotic shame.

"Monsieur Émile?"

"You know him. At any rate, he knows you. He lives with his mother, old Justine, who is one of the most widely known women on the Riviera. She's the proprietor of the Fleurs, at Marseilles, the Sirènes at Nice, two or three houses at Toulon, Béziers, Avignon . . . ."

Had Mr. Pyke realized what sort of houses they were?

"Justine's seventy-nine years old. I thought she was older, for Monsieur Émile admits to being sixty-five. It appears she had him when she was fourteen. She told me so yesterday. They're very quiet, the two of them, and don't see anyone. Look. That's Monsieur Émile you can see in his garden, in the white suit, with the topee. He looks like a white mouse. He has a little boat, like everyone else, but he hardly ever ventures beyond the end of the jetty, where he spends hours happily fishing for *girelle*."

"What's that?" asked Mr. Pyke, whose skin was beginning to dry.

"*Girelle?* An extremely attractive little fish, with red and blue on its back. It's not bad fried, but it's not a serious fish, if you see what I mean."

"I see."

The three of them walked on the sand, along the backs of the houses which faced on to the square.

"There is another local character. We shall probably eat at the next table to him. It's Charlot. Just now, when we landed, he said hello to you, chief. I asked him to stay, and he didn't object. It's curious, actually, that nobody asked to leave. They are all being very calm, very sensible."

"And the big yacht?"

There was indeed an enormous white yacht, not very beautiful, made entirely of metal, which almost filled the harbor.

"The *Alcyon*? It's there all the year round. It belongs to a Lyon businessman, Monsieur Jaureguy, who only uses it for one week in the year, and then it's to go and bathe, all by himself, a stone's throw from the island. There are two sailors on board, two Bretons, who have a pretty easy life."

Was the Englishman expecting to see Maigret taking notes? He watched him smoking his pipe, looking lazily around him, and listening absently to Lechat.

"You see the small green boat, to one side, which has such an odd shape? The cabin is minute, yet there are two people, a man and a girl, living there. They have fixed up a tent by means of the sail, over the deck, and most of the time that's where they sleep. They do their cooking and washing there. Those two aren't regulars. They were found one morning, tied up where you see

them now. The man is called Jef de Greef and is Dutch.
He's a painter. He's only twenty-four. You'll see him.
The girl is called Anna and isn't his wife. I had their papers in my hands. She's eighteen. She was born at Ostend. She's always half-naked and sometimes more
than half. As soon as night falls, you can see both of
them bathing at the end of the jetty without a stitch of
clothing."

Lechat was careful to add for Mr. Pyke's benefit:

"It's true that Mrs. Wilcox, if you can believe the
fishermen, does the same round her yacht."

They were being watched, from a distance. Always
little knots of people who gave the impression of having
nothing else to do all day.

"Another fifty yards further on you can see Marcellin's boat."

From this point the harbor was no longer flanked
with the backs of the houses in the square, but with
villas, most of them surrounded by vegetation.

"They are empty, all except two," Lechat was explaining. "I'll tell you who they belong to. This one
belongs to Monsieur Émile and his mother. I've already
told you about the Minaret."

A supporting wall divided the gardens from the sea.
Each villa had its little landing stage. At one of these, a
local craft, pointed at both ends, about eighteen feet
long, was tied up.

"That's Marcellin's boat."

It was dirty, its deck in disorder. Against the wall was a sort of hearth composed of large stones, a saucepan, some pots blackened by smoke, empty wine bottles.

"Is it true that you knew him, chief? In Paris?"

"In Paris, yes."

"What the local people refuse to believe is that he was born in Le Havre. Everyone is convinced he was a real Southerner. He had the accent. He was a queer fish. He lived in his boat. Now and then he would go for a trip to the continent, as he would call it, which means that he would go and tie his boat up to the jetty at Giens, Saint-Tropez, or Le Lavandou. When the weather was too bad, he would sleep in the hut you can see just above the harbor. That's where the fishermen boil their nets. He had no wants. The butcher would give him a bit of meat occasionally. He didn't fish much, and then only in summer, when he took tourists out. There are a few others like him along the coast."

"Do you have types like that in England, too?" Maigret asked Mr. Pyke.

"It's too cold. We only have the dockside loafers, at the ports."

"Did he drink?"

"White wine. When people needed him to give a hand, they paid him with a bottle of white wine. He used to win it at boules, too, for he was an expert boules player. It was in the boat that I found the letter. I'll give it back to you presently. I've left it at the town hall."

"No other papers?"

"His army book, a photograph of a woman, that's all. It's strange that he should have kept your letter, don't you think?"

Maigret didn't find it so very surprising. He would have liked to talk about it with Mr. Pyke, whose bathing trunks were drying in patches. But that could wait.

"Do you want to see the hut? I've shut it, but I've got the key in my pocket; I shall have to give it back to the fishermen, as they need it."

No huts for the moment. Maigret was hungry. And he was also anxious to see his English colleague in less informal attire. It made him feel awkward, for no very definite reason. He was not accustomed to conducting a case in the company of a man in swimming costume.

He needed another drink of white wine. It was decidedly a tradition on the island. Mr. Pyke went upstairs to dress and returned without a tie, with open collar, like Lechat, and he had found time to procure, probably at the mayor's grocery, a pair of blue canvas espadrilles.

The fishermen, who would have liked to speak to him, still didn't dare. The Arche had two rooms: the room where the bar was, and a smaller one with tables covered with red check tablecloths. These were laid. Two tables away Charlot was busy sampling sea urchins.

Once again he raised a hand in salute as he looked at Maigret. Then he added, idly:

"How goes?"

They had spent several hours, perhaps an entire night, alone together in Maigret's office, five or six years before. The chief inspector had forgotten his real name. Everyone knew him as Charlot.

He did a little bit of everything, procuring girls for licensed brothels in the Midi, smuggling cocaine and certain other goods; he dabbled in racing too, and at election time became one of the most active electioneering agents on the coast.

He was meticulous in his personal appearance, with measured gestures, an imperturbable calm, an ironical little twinkle in his eye.

"Do you like Mediterranean cooking, Mr. Pyke?"

"I don't know it."

"Do you want to try it?"

"With pleasure."

And Paul, the proprietor, suggested:

"Some small birds, to start with? I've a few cooked on the spit, brought in this morning."

They were robins, Paul unfortunately announced as he served the Englishman, who could not help gazing tenderly at his plate.

"As you see, inspector, I've been a good boy."

From where he sat Charlot, without stopping eating, was addressing them in an undertone.

"I've waited for you without being impatient. I haven't even asked the inspector's permission to leave."

A lengthy silence.

"I'm at your service, whenever you like. Paul will tell you that I didn't leave the Arche that evening."

"Are you in such a hurry?"

"What about?"

"To clear yourself."

"I'm just clearing the ground a little, that's all. I'm doing my best to stop you swimming too far out to sea. Because you soon will be swimming. I swim well, but I come from these parts."

"Did you know Marcellin?"

"I've had a drink with him hundreds of times, if that's what you mean. Is it true you've brought someone from Scotland Yard with you?"

He examined Mr. Pyke cynically, like some strange object.

"This is no case for him. It's not a case for you either, if you'll forgive my saying what I think. You know I've always kept clean. We've already had things out between us. There's no hard feelings on either side. What's the fat little sergeant in your office called again? Lucas! How's he getting on, Lucas? Paul! Jojo! . . . Hey! . . ."

As there was no reply, he went toward the kitchen and came back after a few minutes with a plate smelling of garlic mayonnaise.

"I'm not stopping you talking?"

"Not at all."

"If I am, you can just ask me politely to shut my trap. I'm just thirty-four years old. To be exact, it was my birthday yesterday, which means I'm just beginning to feel my age. In my time I've had several chats with your colleagues, either in Paris, or Marseilles, or elsewhere. They haven't always been very polite to me. We haven't always got on together, but there's one thing everyone will tell you: Charlot's never got his hands dirty."

It was true, if one took that to mean he had never killed anyone. He must have had a round dozen convictions to his credit, but for relatively harmless offenses.

"Do you know why I come here regularly? I like the place, obviously, and Paul's a good chap. But there's another reason. Look in the corner, on the left. The fruit machine. It's mine, and I've got around fifty of them from Marseilles to Saint-Raphael. They aren't exactly legal. From time to time, some of your gentlemen turn nasty and remove one or two of them."

Poor Mr. Pyke, who had eaten his little birds to the bitter end, in spite of the softness of his heart! Now he was sniffing the garlic mayonnaise with ill-concealed apprehension.

"You're wondering why I am talking so much, aren't you?"

"I haven't wondered anything yet."

"It's not a habit of mine. But I'll tell you anyway. Here, I mean on the island, there are two characters who are bound to get blamed for the whole affair. They're Émile and me. We've both seen trouble. People are very decent with us, more so as we are openhanded with drinks. They wink at one another. They whisper:

"'They're regular crooks!'

"Or sometimes:

"'Take a look at him. He's quite a lad!'

"Just the same, the moment there's any dirty work it's us they go for.

"I realized that, and that's why I took it easy. I've some pals waiting for me on the coast and I haven't even tried to telephone them. Your little inspector with the dainty manner has been keeping his eye on me and for the last two days has been itching to put me inside. Well! I'll tell you straight, to save you making a blunder: it'd be a big mistake.

"That's all. After which, I'm at your service."

Maigret waited for Charlot to go out, a toothpick at his lips, to ask quietly of his Scotland Yard colleague:

"Does it ever happen over there, that you make friends among your clients?"

"Not in quite the same way."

"How do you mean?"

"We haven't a lot of people like that. Certain things don't happen in quite the same way. Do you follow me?"

Why did Maigret think of Mrs. Wilcox and her young secretary? Indeed certain things did not happen in quite the same way.

"For example, I had dealings, you might call them cordial, for a long time with a notorious jewel thief. We have a lot of jewel thieves. It's something of a national speciality of ours. They are nearly always educated men who come from the best schools, and belong to the smartest clubs. We have the same difficulty as you do with people like this man, or the one called Monsieur Émile: it is to catch them in the act. For four years I kept on the track of the thief I was telling you about. He knew it. We often had a whisky at the bar together.

"We played a number of games of chess together, too."

"And did you get him?"

"Never. In the end we came to a gentleman's agreement. You know the expression? I got rather in his way, so much so, in fact, that last year he wasn't able to try anything on, and he was genuinely hard up. On my side, I wasted a lot of time on his account. I advised him to go and exercise his talents elsewhere. Is that how you say it?"

"Did he go and steal jewels in New York?"

"I rather think he's in Paris," Mr. Pyke corrected him calmly, selecting a toothpick in his turn.

A second bottle of the island's wine, which Jojo had brought without being asked, was more than half-empty. The *patron* came over to suggest:

"A little marc? After the garlic mayonnaise, it's essential."

It was balmy, almost cool in the room, while a heavy sun, humming with flies, beat down on the square.

Charlot, probably for the sake of his digestion, had just begun a game of *pétanque* with a fisherman, and there were half a dozen others to watch them play.

"Will you be doing your interrogations at the town hall?" inquired little Lechat, who didn't seem at all sleepy.

Maigret all but answered:

"What interrogations?"

But he mustn't forget Mr. Pyke, who was swallowing his marc almost without distaste.

"At the town hall, yes . . ."

He would have preferred to go and take a siesta.

3

Monsieur Félicien Jamet, the mayor (of course people just called him Félicien), came along with his key to open the town-hall door for them. Twice before, seeing him cross the square, Maigret had asked himself what it was about his appearance that was abnormal, and he suddenly realized: perhaps because he also sold lamps, kerosene, galvanized wire and nails, Félicien, instead of wearing a grocer's yellowish apron, had taken to the ironmonger's gray smock. He wore it very long, almost down to his ankles. Was he wearing trousers underneath? Or did he leave them off, on account of the heat? The fact remained that if the trousers were there, they were too short to project below the smock, so that the mayor looked as if he were in a nightshirt. More precisely—and the species of skull cap he sported added to the impression—he had something medieval about him, and one had the impression of having seen him before somewhere in a stained-glass window.

"I presume you won't be needing me, gentlemen?"

Standing in the doorway of the dusty room, Maigret and Mr. Pyke looked at one another in some surprise, then looked at Lechat, and finally at Félicien. For on the table, the one used for council meetings and elections, was laid a pine coffin which seemed to have lost something of its brand-newness.

In the most natural way in the world, Monsieur Jamet said to them:

"If you'd like to give me a hand, we can shove it into its corner."

"What is this coffin?" Maigret asked, in surprise.

"It's the municipal coffin. We are obliged by law to provide burial for destitutes and we've only got one carpenter on the island; he's very old and works slowly. In summer, with the heat, the bodies can't be kept waiting."

He spoke of it as of the most banal thing in the world, and Maigret studied the Scotland Yard man out of the corner of his eye.

"Have you many destitute people?"

"We've got one, old Benoît."

"So that the coffin is destined for Benoît?"

"Theoretically. However, last Wednesday it was used to take Marcellin's body to Hyères. Don't worry. It's been disinfected."

There were only some very comfortable folding chairs in the room.

"May I leave you now, gentlemen?"

"Just a moment. Who is Benoît?"

"You must have seen him, or you soon will: he wears his hair down to his shoulders, with a shaggy beard.

Look: through that window, you can see him having his siesta on a bench, near the boules players."

"Is he terribly old?"

"Nobody knows. Nor does he. According to him he's getting on for a hundred, but he must be boasting. He hasn't any papers. His real name isn't known. He landed on the island a very long time ago, when Morin-Barbu, who keeps the café on the corner, was still a young man."

"Where did he come from?"

"That's not known either. From Italy, for certain. Most of them came from Italy. You can usually tell from their way of speaking whether they come from Genoa or the Naples area, but Benoît has a language of his own; he's not easy to understand."

"Is he simple?"

"I beg your pardon?"

"Is he a bit mad?"

"He's as sly as a monkey. Today he looks like a patri-arch. In a few days when the summer trippers begin to arrive, he'll shave his beard and head. He does it every year at the same time. And he starts fishing *mordu*."

Everything had to be learnt.

"*Mordu?*"

"*Mordus* are worms with very hard heads which you find in the sand, on the seashore. Fishermen use them in preference to other bait because they stay on the hook. They fetch a high price. All summer Benoît fishes *mordu* up to his thighs in the water. He used to be a builder, in his young days. It was he that built a good number of the houses on the island. There's nothing else you want, is there, gentlemen?"

Maigret hurriedly opened the window to let the close, musty smell out of the room: it could not have been aired except for July 14, at the same time as they brought out the flags and the chairs.

The chief inspector didn't know exactly what he was doing there. He had no desire to proceed with the interrogations. Why had he said yes when Inspector Lechat had suggested it to him? Through cowardice, on account of Mr. Pyke? Isn't it usual, when one starts a case, to question people? Isn't that the way they do it in England? Would he be taken seriously if he wandered about the island like a man who has nothing else to do?

However, it was the island which interested him at the moment, and not such and such a person in particular. What the mayor had just been saying, for example, set in motion a whole train of thought, so far still nebulous. These men in their little boats who came and went along the coasts, as though quite at home, as though along a boulevard! This did not fit into the picture one had of the sea. It seemed that here the sea had something intimate about it. A few miles from Toulon one met people from Genoa or Naples, perfectly naturally, people in boats, who fished on the way over. Rather like Marcellin. They stopped, and if it suited them, they stayed, perhaps even wrote home for their wife or fiancée to come out?

"Would you like me to bring them in one by one, chief? Who do you want to start with?"

It was all the same to him.

"I see young de Greef crossing the square with his girlfriend. Shall I go and get him?"

He was being rushed, and he didn't dare protest. He had the consolation of noting that his colleague was as sluggish as he was.

"These witnesses you are going to interview," he asked, "are they summoned officially?"

"Not at all. They come because they are willing to. They have the right to reply or not. Most of the time they prefer to reply, but they could always demand the presence of a lawyer."

It must have been spread around that the chief inspector was at the town hall, for groups of people, as in the morning, were forming on the square. Some way away, beneath the eucalyptus trees, Lechat was in animated conversation with a couple, who finally followed him. A mimosa was growing just beside the door and its sweet scent mingled strangely with the musty smell which pervaded the room.

"I suppose, with you, all this is more formal?"

"Not always. Often, in the country or in small towns, the coroner's inquest is held in the back room of an inn."

De Greef seemed all the more fair because his skin was as bronzed as a Tahiti native's. All he wore in the way of clothes was a pair of light-colored shorts and espadrilles, while his companion had a sunsuit tight around her body.

"You wish to speak to me?" he asked, suspiciously.

And Lechat, reassuringly:

"Come in! Chief Inspector Maigret has to question everyone. It's just routine."

The Dutchman spoke French with hardly any accent. He had a net bag in his hand. The two of them were probably going shopping, at the Cooperative, when the inspector had interrupted them.

"Have you been living long aboard your boat?"

"Three years. Why?"

"No reason. You're a painter, they tell me? Do you sell your pictures?"

"When the occasion presents itself."

"Does it often do so?"

"It's rather rare. I sold a canvas to Mrs. Wilcox last week."

"Do you know her well?"

"I met her here."

Lechat came over to speak to Maigret in a low voice. He wanted to know if he should go and fetch Monsieur Émile, and the chief inspector nodded his assent.

"What sort of a person is she?"

"Mrs. Wilcox? She's fantastic."

"What does that mean?"

"Nothing. I might have met her in Montparnasse, for she passes through Paris every winter. We found we had friends in common."

"Have you often been to Montparnasse?"

"I lived in Paris for a year."

"With your boat?"

"We tied up at the Pont Marie."

"Are you rich?"

"I haven't a bean."

"Tell me: exactly how old is your girlfriend?"

"Eighteen and a half."

The latter, her hair falling over her face, her sun-suit molded to her figure, looked like a young savage as she watched Maigret and Mr. Pyke with a blazing eye.

"You aren't married?"

"No."

"Do her parents object?"

"They know she's been living with me."

"For how long?"

"Two and a half years."

"In other words, she was only just sixteen when she became your mistress?"

The word didn't shock either of them.

"Have her parents ever tried to get her back?"

"They've tried several times. She came back."

"So they've given up?"

"They prefer not to think about it anymore."

"What did you live on in Paris?"

"Selling a picture or a drawing now and then. I had friends."

"They lent you money?"

"Sometimes. Other times I was a porter at the vegetable market. Or else I distributed prospectuses."

"Did you already have an urge to come to Porquerolles?"

"I didn't even know of the existence of this island."

"Where were you planning to go?"

"Anywhere, provided there was sun."

"And you expect to go where?"

"Further on."

"Italy?"

"Or somewhere else."

"Did you know Marcellin?"

"He helped to recaulk my boat when it leaked."

"Were you at the Arche de Noé the night he died?"

"We are there almost every night."

"What were you doing?"

"We were playing chess, Anna and I."

"May I inquire, Monsieur de Greef, what is your father's profession?"

"He's a magistrate at Groningen."

"You don't know why Marcellin was killed?"

"I'm not curious."

"Did he speak to you about me?"

"If he did, I didn't hear."

"Do you possess a revolver?"

"What for?"

"You have nothing to say to me?"

"Nothing at all."

"And you, mademoiselle?"

"Nothing, thank you."

He called them back just as they were about to leave.

"One more question. Just now, have you got any money?"

"I told you, I've sold a picture to Mrs. Wilcox."

"You've been aboard her yacht?"

"Several times."

"What do people do aboard yachts?"

"I don't know."

And de Greef added with a hint of contempt:

"You drink. We drank. Is that all?"

Lechat cannot have had to go far to find Monsieur Émile, for the two men were standing in a patch of shade, a few yards from the little town hall. Monsieur Émile looked older than his sixty-five years and he gave an impression of extreme frailty, only moving with great care, as if he were afraid of breaking. He spoke low, economizing every grain of energy.

"Come in, Monsieur Émile. We've met before, I think?"

As Justine's son was eyeing a chair, Maigret went on:

"You can sit down. Did you know Marcellin?"

"Very well."

"You were in constant touch with him? Since when?"

"I couldn't say quite how many years. My mother should be able to remember exactly. Since Ginette's been working for us."

There was a brief silence. It was very strange. One might have thought a bubble had just burst in the peaceful air of the room. Maigret and Mr. Pyke looked at one another. What had Mr. Pyke said as they left Paris? He had mentioned Ginette. He had been surprised—discreetly, as in all things—that the chief inspector had not inquired what had become of her.

Now there was no need for inquiries, or ruses. Quite simply, in his opening remarks, it was Monsieur Émile who mentioned the woman whom, once upon a time, Maigret had sent to a sanatorium.

"You say she works for you? That means, I suppose, in one of your houses."

"At the one in Nice."

"Just a minute, Monsieur Émile. It's a good fifteen years since I met her at the Ternes, and she wasn't a young girl then. If I'm not mistaken, she was well past thirty, and tuberculosis wasn't making her any younger. Now she must be . . ."

"Between forty-five and fifty."

And Monsieur Émile added in the most natural way imaginable:

"It's she who runs the Sirènes, at Nice."

It was better not to look at Mr. Pyke, whose expression of disapproval must have been as ironical as his good education allowed. Hadn't Maigret blushed? At any rate he was conscious of being perfectly ridiculous.

For the fact was that he had on this occasion played the moral reformer. After sending Marcellin to prison, he had turned his attention to Ginette and, just as might happen in a popular novel, had "snatched her from the gutter" to have her put into a sanatorium.

He saw her again clearly, so thin that one wondered how men could allow themselves to be tempted, with feverish eyes and slack mouth.

He said to her:

"You must have treatment, my girl."

And she answered, docilely:

"I'm quite willing, chief inspector. Don't think I enjoy it!"

With a touch of impatience, Maigret now asked, looking Monsieur Émile straight in the face:

"You're sure it's the same woman? At that time she was riddled with consumption."

"She kept up her cure for a few years."

"Did she stay with Marcellin?"

"She hardly saw him, you know. She's very busy. She sent him a money order from time to time. Not large sums. He didn't need them."

Monsieur Émile took a eucalyptus pill from a small box, and sucked it gravely.

"Used he to go and see her in Nice?"

"I don't think so. It's a high-class establishment. You probably know it."

"Was it because of her that Marcellin came to the Midi?"

"I don't know. He was a queer fish."

"Is Ginette in Nice at the moment?"

"She rang us up from Hyères this morning. She saw what happened from the papers. She's in Hyères seeing to the funeral."

"Do you know where she's staying?"

"At the Hôtel des Palmes."

"You were at the Arche the evening of the murder?"

"I went there for my tisane."

"Did you leave before Marcellin?"

"Certainly. I never go to bed after ten o'clock."

"Did you hear him speaking of me?"

"Perhaps. I paid no attention. I'm a bit hard of hearing."

"What are your relations like with Charlot?"

"I know him, but I don't see a lot of him."

"Why?"

Monsieur Émile was visibly striving to explain a delicate matter.

"We don't move in the same circles, if you see what I mean?"

"He's never worked for your mother?"

"He may once or twice have found staff for her."

"Has he been going straight?"

"I think so."

"Did Marcellin find people for you too?"

"No. He didn't go in for that."

"You know nothing?"

"Nothing at all. I hardly concern myself with business matters any longer. My health won't allow me."

What was Mr. Pyke thinking of all this? Are there
Monsieur Émiles in England as well?

"I think I might go and have a chat with your
mother."

"You'll be very welcome, inspector."

Lechat was outside, this time in the company of a
young man in white flannel trousers, a blue striped
blazer, and a yachting cap.

"Monsieur Philippe de Moricourt," he announced.
"He was just landing with the dinghy."

"You wish to speak to me, inspector?"

He was in his thirties, and, contrary to what one
might have expected, he wasn't even good-looking.

"I presume this is mere formality?"

"Sit down."

"Is it essential? I loathe sitting down."

"Stay standing up then. You're Mrs. Wilcox's secretary?"

"A nominal title, of course. Let us say that I am her
guest and that, as between friends, I sometimes act as
her secretary."

"Is Mrs. Wilcox writing her memoirs?"

"No. Why do you ask?"

"Does she have anything to do with her whisky firm
herself?"

"Nothing whatever."

"Do you write her private letters?"

"I can't see what you are driving at."

"At nothing at all, Monsieur Moricourt."

"De Moricourt."

"If you insist. I was only trying to get some idea of your work."

"Mrs. Wilcox is no longer young."

"Exactly."

"I don't get you."

"Never mind. Tell me, Monsieur de Moricourt—that's right, isn't it?—where you made Mrs. Wilcox's acquaintance?"

"Is this an interrogation?"

"It's whatever you like to call it."

"Am I obliged to answer?"

"You can wait until I summon you formally."

"Am I regarded as a suspect?"

"Everyone is suspect, and no one is."

The young man considered for a few moments, threw his cigarette through the open doorway.

"I met her at the casino at Cannes."

"A long time ago?"

"A little over a year."

"Are you a gambler?"

"I used to be. That's how I lost my money."

"Did you have a lot?"

"The question strikes me as indiscreet."

"Did you have a job before?"

"I was attached to the office of a minister."

"Who was doubtless a friend of your family's?"

"How did you know?"

"Do you know young de Greef?"

"He's been on board several times, and we bought a canvas from him."

"You mean that Mrs. Wilcox bought a canvas from him?"

"That's right. I beg your pardon."

"Had Marcellin been on board the *North Star* as well?"

"Occasionally."

"As a guest?"

"It's difficult to explain, inspector. Mrs. Wilcox is a very generous person."

"I imagine so."

"Everything interests her, especially in the Mediterranean, which she loves, and it abounds in colorful characters. Marcellin was undeniably one himself."

"He was given drinks?"

"Everyone is given drinks."

"You were at the Arche on the night of the crime?"

"We were with the major."

"Another colorful character, no doubt?"

"Mrs. Wilcox used to know him in England. It was a social connection."

"Were you drinking champagne?"

"The major drinks nothing but champagne."

"Were the three of you very merry?"

"We behaved perfectly well."

"Did Marcellin join in with your party?"

"Everyone more or less joined in. You haven't met Major Bellam yet?"

"Doubtless it won't be long before I have that pleasure."

"He's generosity itself. When he comes to the Arche . . ."

"And he often goes there?"

"That is correct. As I was saying, he seldom fails to offer drinks all round. Everyone comes to have a drink with him. He's been living on the island such a long time that he knows the children by their Christian names."

"So Marcellin came over to your table. He drank a glass of champagne."

"No. He had a horror of champagne. He used to say it was only fit for girls. We had a bottle of white wine fetched up for him."

"Did he sit down?"

"Of course."

"There were other people seated at your table? Charlot for example?"

"Oh yes."

"You know his profession, if one can use the term?"

"He doesn't try to hide the fact that he is a crook. He's a character too."

"And, in that capacity, he was sometimes invited on board?"

"I don't think, inspector, that there's anyone on the island who hasn't been."

"Even Monsieur Émile?"

"Not him."

"Why?"

"I don't know. I don't think we've ever even spoken to him. He's something of a hermit."

"And he doesn't drink."

"That's so."

"Because you drink a lot, on board, don't you?"

"At times. I presume it's allowed?"

"Was Marcellin at your table when he started talking about me?"

"Probably. I don't remember exactly. He was telling stories, as usual. Mrs. Wilcox liked to hear him tell stories. He talked about his years in a penal settlement."

"He never went to a penal settlement."

"In that case, he invented it."

"To amuse Mrs. Wilcox. So he talked about prison. And I was brought into the story? Was he drunk?"

"He was never entirely sober, especially in the evening. Wait. He said he had been convicted because of a woman."

"Ginette?"

"Maybe. I seem to recall the name. It was then, I think, that he claimed that you had looked after her. Someone murmured: 'Maigret—he's just a copper like the rest of them.' Forgive me."

"Not at all. Carry on."

"That's all. At that he started singing your praises, saying you were a friend of his and that for him a friend was sacred. If I remember rightly, Charlot teased him and he became even more worked up."

"Can you tell me exactly how it finished?"

"It's difficult. It was late."

"Who was the first to leave?"

"I don't know. Paul had closed the shutters a long time before. He was sitting at our table. We had a final bottle. I think we left together."

"Who?"

"The major left us in the square to go back to his villa. Charlot, who sleeps at the Arche, stayed behind. Mrs. Wilcox and I went off to the landing stage, where we had left the dinghy."

"Did you have a sailor with you?"

"No. We usually leave them on board. There was a strong mistral blowing and the sea was choppy. Marcellin offered to take us."

"So he was with you when you set off."

"Yes. He stayed on shore. He must have gone back to the hut."

"In short, you and Mrs. Wilcox were the last people to see him alive?"

"Apart from the murderer."

"Did you have difficulty getting back to the yacht?"

"How did you know?"

"You told me the sea was rough."

"We arrived soaking wet, with six inches of water in the dinghy."

"Did you go straight to bed?"

"I made some grog to warm us up, after which we played a game of gin rummy."

"I beg your pardon?"

"It's a card game."

"What time was this?"

"Around two in the morning. We never go to bed early."

"You didn't hear or see anything unusual?"

"The mistral prevented us from hearing anything."

"Are you thinking of coming to the Arche this evening?"

"Probably."

"Thank you."

Maigret and Mr. Pyke remained alone together for a moment or two, and the chief inspector gazed at his colleague with large, sleepy eyes. He had the feeling that it was all futile, that he ought to have tackled it differently. For example, he would have liked to be on the square, in the sunshine, smoking his pipe and watching the boules players, who had started a big match; he would have liked to roam about the harbor watching the fishermen repairing their nets; he would have liked to know all the Gallis and the Morins whom Lechat had just touched on in conversation with him.

"I believe that in your country, Mr. Pyke, investigations are carried out in a very orderly fashion, aren't they?"

"It all depends. For example, after a crime committed two years ago near Brighton, one of my colleagues stayed eleven weeks in an inn, spending his days fishing and his evenings drinking ale with the locals."

That was exactly what Maigret would have liked to do, and what he was not doing on account of this very Mr. Pyke! When Lechat came in, he was in a bad temper.

"The major wouldn't come," he announced. "He's in his garden, doing nothing. I told him you asked him to step along here. He replied that if you wanted to see him, you had only to go and drink a bottle with him."

"He's within his rights."

"Who do you want to question now?"

"Nobody. I'd like you to telephone to Hyères. I presume there is a telephone at the Arche? Ask for Ginette, at the Hôtel des Palmes. Tell her from me that I would be glad if she would come and have a chat with me."

"Where shall I find you?"

"I don't know. Probably at the harbor."

They walked slowly across the square, Mr. Pyke and he, and people followed them with their eyes. One might have thought it was with some distrust, but it was only that they didn't know how to behave in the presence of the famous Maigret. The latter, on his side, felt an *estranger*, as they say locally. But he knew that it would not take much for every one of them to start talking freely, perhaps too freely.

"Don't you find you have the impression of being miles away, Mr. Pyke? Look! That's France you can see over there, twenty minutes away by boat, and I'm as lost as if I were in the heart of Africa or South America."

Some children stopped playing, so as to examine them. They reached the Grand Hôtel, came in sight of the harbor, and Inspector Lechat was back with them already.

"I couldn't get her on the line," he announced. "She's left."

"Has she gone back to Nice?"

"Probably not, as she told the hotel that she'd be back tomorrow morning in time for the burial."

The jetty, the small boats of all colors, the big yacht blocking the harbor, the *North Star*, far out, near a rocky promontory, and people watching another boat arriving:

"That's the *Cormorant*," Lechat explained. "In other words, it's just about five o'clock."

A youth, with a cap bearing the words "Grand Hôtel" in gold letters, was waiting for the guests-to-be beside a barrow intended for luggage. The small white boat approached, with silvered mustaches given it by the sea, and Maigret was not long in spotting, in the bows, a female figure.

"Probably Ginette, coming to meet you," the inspector said. "Everyone at Hyères must know you are here."

It was a strange sensation to see the people in the boat, slowly growing in size, becoming more clearly defined as on a photographic plate. Above all, it was distressing to see a woman, with Ginette's features, very fat, very respectable, all in silk, all made up, and, no doubt, heavily scented.

Truth to tell, when Maigret had met her in the Brasserie des Ternes, was he not himself more slim, and wasn't she feeling at that moment just as disappointed as he, while she watched him from the deck of the *Cormorant*?

She had to be helped down the gangway. Apart from her there was no one on board besides Baptiste, the captain, except the dumb sailor and the postman. The lad with the gold-braided cap tried to take possession of her luggage.

"To the Arche de Noé!" she said.

She went up to Maigret, hesitated, perhaps on account of Mr. Pyke, whom she didn't know.

"They told me you were here. I thought you might like to speak to me. Poor Marcel! . . ."

She didn't say Marcellin, like the others. She didn't affect any great sorrow. She had become a mature person, sober and calm, with a glimmer of a slightly disillusioned smile.

"Are you staying at the Arche as well?"

It was Lechat who took her case. She seemed to know the island and walked quietly, without haste, like one who easily gets out of breath, or who isn't made for the open air.

"*Le Petit Var* says it's because he mentioned you that he was killed. Do you believe it?"

Now and again she cast a glance, at once curious and anxious, at Mr. Pyke.

"You can talk in front of him. He's a friend, an English colleague who's come to stay a few days with me."

She gave the Scotland Yard man a very ladylike smile and sighed with a glance at the stout profile of the chief inspector:

"I've changed, haven't I?"

her inspector.

4

It was strange to see her overcome with a feeling of
modesty, and holding her dress tight against her because the stairway was steep and Maigret was coming
up behind her.

She had come into the Arche as she would into her
own house, had said in the most natural way in the world:

"Have you a room left for me, Paul?"

"You'll have to put up with the little room beside the
bathroom."

Then she had turned to Maigret.

"Would you like to come up for a moment, inspector?"

These words would have had a double meaning in
the house she ran at Nice, but not here. Nonetheless
she showed her scorn for Maigret's hesitation, who was
keeping up his game of hiding nothing of the case
from Mr. Pyke. For a moment, her smile was almost
professional.

"I'm not dangerous, you know."

For some extraordinary reason, the Scotland Yard
inspector spoke English, perhaps out of delicacy. He
said only one word, to his French colleague.

"Please . . ."

On the stairway Jojo went in front with the suitcase. She wore a very short dress and you could see the pink slip enveloping her little behind. No doubt that was what had given Ginette the idea of holding her dress tightly against her.

Apart from the bed there was only a straw-bottomed chair to sit on, for it was the smallest of the rooms, poorly lighted by one attic window. Ginette took off her hat, sank onto the edge of the bed with a sigh of relief and immediately removed her extremely high-heeled shoes, and, through the silk of her stockings, caressed her aching toes.

"Are you annoyed that I asked you to come upstairs? There's no place to talk downstairs, and I hadn't the energy to walk. Look at my ankles: they're all swollen. You can smoke your pipe, inspector."

She was not completely at her ease. It was obvious that she was talking for the sake of talking, to gain time.

"Are you very cross with me?"

Although he understood, he gained time himself as well, by countering:

"What about?"

"I know perfectly well that you're disappointed. But it isn't really my fault. Thanks to you, I spent the happiest years of my life in the san. I didn't have anything to worry about. There was a doctor rather like you who was extremely kind to me. He brought me books. I used to read all day. Before going there I was ignorant. Then, when there was something I couldn't understand, he would explain it to me. Have you got a cigarette? Never mind. Besides, it's better for me not to smoke . . .

"I stayed five years at the san, and I had come to believe I'd spend my whole life there. I liked the idea. Unlike the others, I had no desire to go out.

"When they told me I was cured and could go, I can tell you I was more afraid than glad. From where we were, we could see the valley almost always covered with a kind of mist, sometimes with thick clouds, and I was afraid of going down into it again. I would have liked to have stayed as a nurse, but I hadn't the necessary knowledge, and I wasn't strong enough to do the housework or be a kitchen maid.

"What could I have done, down there? I had got into the habit of having three meals a day. I knew that with Justine I should have that."

"Why did you come today?" asked Maigret in a rather cold voice.

"Haven't I just told you? I first went to Hyères. I didn't want poor Marcel to be buried without anyone to follow the hearse."

"Were you still in love with him?"

She showed slight embarrassment.

"I think I really was in love with him, you know. I talked about him a lot to you, in the old days, when you took me up after his arrest. He wasn't a bad man, you know. Underneath he was really rather innocent, I'd even say shy. And just because he was shy he wanted to be like the others. Only he exaggerated. Up there I understood everything."

"And you stopped loving him?"

"I didn't love him anymore in the same way. I saw other people. I could make comparisons. The doctor helped me to understand."

"Were you in love with the doctor?"

She laughed, a little nervously.

"I think in a sanatorium people are always more or less in love with their doctors."

"Did Marcel write to you?"

"Now and then."

"Was he hoping to take up the old life with you again?"

"At first, yes, I think so. Then he changed, too. We didn't change in the same way, the two of us. He grew old very quickly, almost overnight. I don't know if you saw him again. Before, he was smart, particular about his appearance. He was proud. It all started when he came to the Riviera, quite by chance."

"Was it he who made you go into service with Justine and Émile?"

"No. I knew Justine by name. I applied to her. She took me on trial, as an assistant manageress, as I wasn't fit for anything else. I was operated on four times up there, and my body is covered with scars."

"I asked you why you had come today."

He came relentlessly back to this question.

"When I found out that you were on the case, I thought you would remember me and try to get hold of me. That would probably have taken some time."

"If I understand you correctly, since you came out of the sanatorium you had no further relations with Marcel, but you sent him money orders?"

"Occasionally. I wanted him to enjoy himself a little. He wouldn't show it but he went through some bad patches."

"Did he tell you so?"

"He told me he was a failure, that he always had been a failure, and that he hadn't even been able to become a real crook."

"Was it in Nice that he told you this?"

"He never came to see me at the Sirènes. He knew it was forbidden."

"Here?"

"Yes."

"Do you often come to Porquerolles?"

"Nearly every month. Justine's too old, now, to inspect her establishments herself. Monsieur Émile has never liked traveling."

"Do you sleep here, at the Arche?"

"Always."

"Why doesn't Justine give you a room? The villa is large enough."

"She never has women sleeping under her roof."

He sensed that he was reaching the sensitive spot, but Ginette wasn't giving in completely yet.

"Is she afraid for her son?" he asked jokingly, as he lit a fresh pipe.

"Strange though it may seem, it's the truth. She has always made him live tied to her apron strings and that is why he has got a girl's character rather than a man's. At his age she still treats him like a child. He can't do anything without her permission."

"Does he like women?"

"He's more afraid of them. I mean in general. He's not keen, you know. He's never had good health. He spends his time looking after himself, taking pills, reading medical books."

"What else is there, Ginette?"

"What do you mean?"

"Why have you come here today?"

"But I've told you."

"No."

"I thought you would be wondering about Monsieur Émile and his mother."

"Explain."

"You aren't like the other detectives, but even so! When something fishy happens, it's always people of a certain type that are suspected."

"And you intended to tell me that Monsieur Émile had nothing to do with Marcel's death?"

"I wanted to explain to you . . ."

"Explain what?"

"We remained good friends, Marcel and me, but there was no question of living together. He no longer thought about that. I don't think he even wanted it. Do you understand? He was enjoying the kind of life he had made for himself. He no longer had any relations with the underworld. Look I saw Charlot, just now . . ."

"You know him?"

"I've met him here several times. We even ate occasionally at the same table. He's found girls for me."

"Were you expecting him to be at Porquerolles today?"

"No. I swear I'm speaking the truth. It's your way of putting questions that upsets me. Before, you used to trust me. You were even a little sorry for me. It's true I've no longer anything to be sorry about, have I? I haven't got TB now!"

"Do you make a lot of money?"

"Not so much as you might think. Justine is very tightfisted. So is her son. I don't go without anything, of course. I even put a little aside, but not enough to retire on."

"You were telling me about Marcel."

"I can't remember what I was saying. Oh yes! How can I explain? When you knew him he used to try to play the tough guy. In Paris he was always going to bars where you meet people like Charlot, and even killers. He wanted to look as though he belonged to their gangs and they didn't take him seriously . . ."

"He was a half-and-half, eh?"

"Well, he grew out of it. He grew up seeing those types, and lived in his boat or in his hut. He drank a lot.

He always found some means of getting a drink. My money orders used to help him. I know what people think when a man like him is killed . . ."

"That is?"

"You know it, too. People imagine it's an underworld affair, a settling of accounts, or a revenge. But that isn't the case."

"That's what you really came to say, isn't it?"

"For the last few minutes I've lost my train of thought. You've changed so much! I'm sorry. I don't mean physically . . ."

He smiled, in spite of himself, at her confusion.

"In the old days, even in your office in the Quai des Orfèvres, you didn't remind one of a policeman."

"You're really afraid that I'm going to suspect the old cons? You aren't in love with Charlot, by any chance?"

"Certainly not. I'd be pretty hard put to it to be in love with anyone after all the operations I've been through. I'm not a woman anymore, if you must know. And Charlot doesn't interest me any more than the others."

"Tell me the rest now."

"What makes you think there is anything else? I give you my word of honor that I don't know who killed poor Marcel."

"But you know who didn't kill him."

"Yes."

"You know whom I might be led to suspect."

"After all, you'll find out for yourself one of these days, if you haven't already done so. I would have said so to start off with if you hadn't questioned me so drily. I'm going to marry Monsieur Émile. There!"

"When?"

"When Justine dies."

"Why do you have to wait until she isn't there anymore?"

"I tell you she's jealous of all women. It's because of her that he hasn't married or even been known to have any mistresses. When, from time to time, he needed a woman, it was she who chose him the least dangerous one, and she never ceased giving him advice. Now all that's over."

"For whom?"

"For him, of course!"

"And yet he's still contemplating marriage?"

"Because he has a horror of being left alone. As long as his mother is alive, he is content. She looks after him like a baby. But she hasn't much time left. A year at the outside."

"Did the doctor say so?"

"She's got cancer and she is too old to have an operation. As for him he always imagines he's going to die. He has fits of breathlessness several times a day, doesn't dare stir, as if the least movement might be fatal . . ."

"So he's asked you to marry him?"

"Yes. He made sure I was fit enough to look after him. He's even had me examined by several doctors. Needless to say Justine knows nothing, or she would have thrown me out a long time ago."

"And Marcel?"

"I told him."

"What was his reaction?"

"None. He thought I was right to provide for my old age. I think it pleased him to know that I would come to live here."

"Monsieur Émile wasn't jealous of Marcel?"

"Why would he have been jealous? I've already told you there was nothing between us anymore."

"In short, this is what you were so anxious to talk to me about?"

"I thought of all the assumptions you would arrive at which don't correspond to reality."

"For example that Marcel might have been able to blackmail Monsieur Émile, and the latter, to get him out of the way . . ."

"Marcel never blackmailed anyone, and Monsieur Émile would rather die of hunger than strangle a chicken!"

"Of course you haven't been on to the island these last few days?"

"It's easy to check up."

"Because you hadn't left the house in Nice, had you? It's an excellent alibi."

"Do I need one?"

"According to what you said just now—I am speaking as a policeman. Marcel, despite everything, could have been in your way. Especially as Monsieur Émile is a big fish, a very big fish. Supposing he does marry you, he would leave you, on his death, a considerable fortune."

"Quite considerable, yes! I wonder now if I was right to come. I wasn't expecting you to speak to me like that. I've admitted everything to you, frankly."

Her eyes were shining, as though she were on the verge of tears, and it was an old face, badly patched up and disfigured with a childish pout, that Maigret beheld.

"You can do what you like. I don't know who killed Marcel. It's a catastrophe."

"Especially for him."

"For him too, yes. But he's at rest. Are you going to arrest me?"

She had said this with the shadow of a smile, although one could feel that she was anxious, more serious than she wanted to appear.

"For the moment I have no such intention."

"Can I go to the funeral tomorrow morning? If you like, I'll come straight back afterwards. All you have to do is send a boat for me at Giens Point."

"Perhaps."

"You won't say anything to Justine?"

"Not before it's strictly necessary and I don't envisage the necessity."

"Are you cross with me?"

"Of course not."

"Yes. I felt it straightaway, before leaving the *Cormorant*, from the moment I saw you. I recognized you. I was moved, because it was a whole period of my life coming back to me."

"A period of regret?"

"Perhaps. I don't know. I sometimes wonder."

She rose with a sigh, without putting on her shoes again. She wanted to unlace her stays and was waiting for the chief inspector to leave before doing so.

"You must do as you wish," she sighed finally, as he was putting his hand to the doorknob.

And he felt something like a pang at leaving her all alone, aging, anxious, in the little bedroom into which the setting sun penetrated through the attic window, casting everywhere, on the painted wallpaper and the counterpane, a pink hue, like rouge.

"A white wine, Monsieur Maigret!"

Noise, all of a sudden, and movement. The boules players, who had finished their game on the square, were crowding round the bar and speaking at the tops of their voices, with strong accents. In a corner of the dining room, near the window, Mr. Pyke was at a table opposite Jef de Greef, and the two men were deeply engrossed in a game of chess.

Beside them, on the bench, Anna was sitting smoking a cigarette at the end of a long cigarette holder. She had dressed. She wore a little cotton frock under which one sensed she was as naked as beneath her sunsuit. She had a well-rounded body, extremely feminine, so expressly made for caressing that despite oneself one imagined her in bed.

De Greef had put on a pair of gray flannel trousers and a sailor's jersey with blue and white stripes. On his feet he wore rope-soled espadrilles, like practically everyone else on the island, and they were the first thing that strict Mr. Pyke had bought.

Maigret looked round for the inspector, but didn't see him. He was obliged to accept the glass of wine which Paul was pushing toward him, and the people at the bar squeezed themselves together to make room for him.

"Well, inspector?"

They were appealing to him, and he knew that in a few minutes the ice would be broken. Probably the islanders had been waiting ever since the morning for this particular moment to make his acquaintance? There was quite a crowd of them, about ten at the least, most of them in fishermen's clothes. Two or three had a more bourgeois look, probably retired on a modest income.

Never mind what Mr. Pyke might think. He had to have a drink.

"You like our island wine?"

"Very much."

"But the papers claim you only drink beer. Marcellin said it wasn't true, that you didn't pull a face at a jug of calvados. Poor Marcellin! Your health, inspector . . ."

Paul, the *patron*, who knew how these things develop, kept the bottle in his hand.

"It's true, he was a friend of yours?"

"I knew him once, yes. He wasn't a bad fellow."

"Certainly not. Are the papers right, too, when they say he came from Le Havre?"

"Certainly."

"With his accent?"

"When I knew him, some fifteen years ago, he hadn't got any accent."

"You hear that, Titin? What have I always said?"

Four rounds . . . five rounds . . . and words being bandied about rather at random, for the sake of saying them, like children throwing balls into the air.

"What do you feel like eating this evening, inspector? There is bouillabaisse, of course. But perhaps you don't like bouillabaisse?"

He swore that he liked nothing better, and everyone was delighted. It wasn't the moment to get to know personally the people who surrounded him and formed a rather confused mass.

"You like pastis as well, the real stuff, which is banned? A pastis all round, Paul! I insist! The inspector won't say anything . . ."

Charlot was sitting on the terrace, with a pastis in front of him, busy reading a paper.

"Have you got any ideas yet?"

"Ideas about what?"

"Well, about the murderer! Morin-Barbu, who was born on the island and hasn't left it for seventy-seven years, has never heard of anything like it. There have been people drowned. A woman from the North, five or six years back, tried to do away with herself by swallowing sleeping tablets. An Italian sailor, in the course of an argument, stabbed Baptiste in the arm. But a crime, never, inspector! Here even the bad ones become as gentle as lambs."

Everybody there was laughing, trying to talk, for what counted was to talk, to say anything, chat over your drink with the famous inspector.

"You'll understand better when you've been here a few days. What you ought to do is to come and spend your holidays here with your wife. We'd teach you to play boules. Isn't that right, Casimir? Casimir won the *Petit Provençal* championship last year, and you know what that means."

From the pink it had been a short while ago, the church at the far end of the square was becoming violet; the sky was gently turning a pale green and the men began to depart one after the other; now and again a shrill woman's voice could be heard calling in the distance:

"Hey, Jules! . . . The soup's ready . . ."

Or else a small boy would come boldly in to look for his father and pull him by the hand.

"Well, aren't we going to have a game?"

"It's too late."

It was explained to Maigret that after the game of boules it was cards, but that the latter hadn't taken place because of him. The sailor from the *Cormorant*, a dumb colossus with immense bare feet, who smiled at the chief inspector with all his teeth, now and again raised his glass and made a strange gobbling noise which took the place of: "*Here's to you!*"

"Do you want to eat straightaway?"

"Have you seen the inspector?"

"He went out while you were upstairs. He didn't say anything. That's his way. He's marvelous, you know. In the three days he's been ferreting about the island, he knows almost as much as I do about all the families."

Leaning forward, Maigret could see that the de Greefs had left and the Englishman was alone in front of the chessboard.

"We eat in half an hour," he announced.

Paul asked him in a low voice, indicating the Scotland Yard detective:

"Do you think he likes our cooking?"

A few minutes later Maigret and his colleague went out for a walk and, quite naturally, walked toward the harbor. They had fallen into the habit. The sun had disappeared, and there was a feeling, as it were, of an immense release in the air. The noises were no longer the same. One could hear the faint lapping of the water against the stone of the jetty, and the stone had become a harder gray, like the rocks. The greenery was dark, almost black, mysterious, and a torpedo boat with a huge number painted in white on the hull slid silently toward the open sea, at what appeared to be a giddy speed.

"I just beat him," Mr. Pyke had declared at the outset. "He's very good, very much his own master."

"It was he that suggested the game?"

"I had taken the chessmen, to practice" (he didn't add: while you were upstairs with Ginette), "not expecting to find an opponent. He sat down at the next table with his girlfriend and I realized, from his way of looking at the pieces, that he wanted to pit his wits against mine."

After this there had been a long silence and now the two men were strolling along the jetty. Near the white yacht there was a little boat, the name of which could be seen on the stern: *Fleur d'amour*.

It was de Greef's boat, and the couple were on board. There was a light under the roof, in a cabin just wide enough for two, where it was impossible to stand up. A noise of spoons and crockery was coming from within. A meal was in progress.

When the detectives had passed the yacht, Mr. Pyke spoke again, slowly, with his habitual precision.

"He's the sort of son good families hate to have. Actually you can't have many specimens in France."

Maigret was quite taken aback, for it was the first time, since he had known him, that his colleague had expressed general ideas. Mr. Pyke seemed a little embarrassed himself, as though overcome with shame.

"What makes you think we have hardly any in France?"

"I mean not of that type, exactly."

He picked his words with great care, standing still at the end of the jetty, facing the mountains which could be seen on the mainland.

"I rather think that in your country, a boy from a good family can commit some *bêtises*, as you say, so as to have a good time, to enjoy himself with women or cars, or to gamble in the casino. Do your bad boys play chess? I doubt it. Do they read Kant, Schopenhauer, Nietzsche, and Kierkegaard? It's unlikely, isn't it? They only want to live their life without waiting for their inheritance."

They leaned against the wall which ran along one side of the jetty, and the calm surface of the water was occasionally troubled by a fish jumping.

"De Greef does not belong to that category of bad characters. I don't think he even wants to have money. He's almost a pure anarchist. He has revolted against everything he has known, against everything he's been taught, against his magistrate of a father and his bourgeois mother, against his hometown, against the customs of his own country."

He broke off, half-blushing.

"I beg your pardon . . ."

"Go on, please."

"We only exchanged a few words, the two of us, but I think I have understood him, because there are a lot of young people like that in my country, in all countries, probably, where morals are very strict. That's why I said just now that one probably doesn't come across a vast number of that type in France. Here there isn't any hypocrisy. Perhaps there isn't enough."

Was he alluding to the surroundings, the world the two of them had been plunged in since their arrival, to the Monsieur Émiles, the Charlots, the Ginettes, who lived among the others without being singled out for opprobrium?

Maigret felt a little anxious, a little piqued. Without being attacked, he was stung by an urge to defend himself.

"By way of protest," pursued Mr. Pyke, "these young people reject everything *en bloc*, the good and the bad. Look, he has taken a young girl away from her family. She's sweet, very desirable. I don't think, however, that it was from desire for her that he did it. It was because she belonged to a good family, because she was a girl who used to go to Mass every Sunday with her mother. It was because her father is probably an austere and high-minded gentleman. Also because he was taking a big risk in carrying her off. But, of course, I may be quite wrong."

"I don't think so."

"There are some people who, when in a clean and elegant setting, feel the need to defile. De Greef feels the need to defile life, to defile anything. And even to defile his girlfriend."

This time Maigret was astounded. He was bowled over, as they say, for he realized that Mr. Pyke had been thinking the same thing as he had. When de Greef had admitted having been several times on board the *North Star*, it had immediately occurred to him that it was not only to drink, but that more intimate and less admissible relations existed between the two couples.

"They are very dangerous fellows," Mr. Pyke concluded.

He added:

"Perhaps they are very unhappy too?"

Then, probably finding the silence a little too solemn, he said in a lighter tone:

"He speaks perfect English, you know. He hasn't even got an accent. I shouldn't be surprised if he went to one of our public schools."

It was time to go to dinner. It was long past the half hour. The darkness was almost complete, and the boats in the harbor were swaying to the rhythm of the sea's breathing. Maigret emptied his pipe and knocked it against his heel, hesitated to fill another. Going past, he studied the Dutchman's little boat closely.

Had Mr. Pyke just spoken for the sake of speaking? Had he, in his own way, wanted to convey some sort of message?

It was difficult, if not impossible, to tell. His French was perfect, too perfect, and yet the two men did not speak the same language, their thoughts followed different channels in their passage through the brain.

"They're very dangerous, those fellows," the Scotland Yard inspector had emphasized.

There was no doubt that he would not have wished, for anything in the world, even to appear to be intervening in Maigret's case. He hadn't asked him any questions about what had happened in Ginette's room. Was he under the impression that his colleague was hiding something from him, that Maigret was trying to cheat? Or worse still, after what he had just said about the customs of the French, did he imagine that Maigret and Ginette . . . ?

The chief inspector grunted:

"She told me of her engagement to Monsieur Émile. It has to be kept secret, because of old Justine, who would attempt to stop the marriage, even after her death."

He noticed that by contrast with the telling phrases of Mr. Pyke his speech was vague, his ideas even vaguer.

In a few words the Englishman had said what he had to say. From half an hour spent with de Greef, he had formulated definite ideas, not only about the latter, but on the world in general.

As for Maigret he would have been hard put to it to express a single idea. It was quite different. He sensed something. He sensed a whole heap of things, as he always did at the start of a case, but he couldn't have said in what form this mist of ideas would sooner or later resolve itself.

It was rather humiliating. It was a loss of face. He felt himself heavy and dull-witted beside the clear silhouette of his colleague.

"She's a strange girl," he mumbled, in spite of everything.

That was all he could find to say of someone he had met before, whose whole life story he almost knew, and who had spoken to him openly.

A strange girl! She attracted him in some ways, and in others she disappointed him, as she had herself sensed perfectly well.

Perhaps, later on, he would have a definite opinion about her?

After a single game of chess and a few remarks exchanged over the board, Mr. Pyke had made a definitive analysis of his opponent's character.

Was it not as though the Englishman had won the first rubber?

5

He had thought about the smell straightaway, when he still imagined he was going to go to sleep at once. In actual fact, there were several smells. The principal one, the smell of the house, which one sniffed immediately on crossing the threshold of the café, he had been trying to analyze since that morning, for it was a smell which was unfamiliar to him. It struck him every time as he went in, and, each time, he would dilate his nostrils. There was a basis of wine of course, with a touch of *anis*, then the kitchen odors. And, since it was a Mediterranean kitchen, with foundations of garlic, red peppers, oil, and saffron, this made it differ from the usual smells.

But what was the point of worrying about all this? His eyes closed, he wanted to sleep. It was no use calling to mind all the Marseillais or Provençal restaurants where he happened to have eaten, in Paris or elsewhere. The smell wasn't the same, let it rest at that. All he had to do was sleep. He had had enough to drink to plunge into a leaden sleep.

Hadn't he been to sleep, immediately after lying down? The window was open and a noise had intrigued him; he had finally realized it was the rustling of leaves in the trees on the square.

Strictly speaking, the smell downstairs could be compared with that of a small bar, in Cannes, kept by a fat woman, where he had once been on a case and had idled away many hours.

The one in the bedroom was unlike anything. What was there in the mattress? Was it, as in Brittany, seaweed, which gave off the iodized smell of the sea? Other people had been in the bed before him, and he thought at odd moments that he could detect the smell of the oil with which women smear themselves before sunbathing.

He turned over heavily. It was at least the tenth time, and there was still someone about, opening a door, walking down the passage, and going into one of the lavatories. There was nothing extraordinary about that, but it seemed to him that far more people were going there than there were in the house. Then he began counting the occupants of the Arche. Paul and his wife slept over his head, in an attic which one reached by a sort of ladder. As for Jojo, he didn't know where she slept. At any rate there was no room for her on the first floor.

She, too, had a special smell of her own. It came partly from her oiled hair, partly from her body and clothes, and it was at once vague and spicy, not at all disagreeable. This smell had distracted him while she was talking to him.

Another case where Mr. Pyke might have thought Maigret was cheating. The chief inspector had gone up to his bedroom for a moment, after dinner, to wash his teeth and hands. He had left the door open, and without his hearing, her feet making no sound on the floor, Jojo had come in and stood framed in the doorway. How old could she be? Sixteen? Twenty? She had the look, at once admiring and timorous, of girls who go to the stage door of theaters to beg for autographs. Maigret impressed her, because he was famous.

"Have you got something to say to me, my girl?"

She had closed the door behind her, which he hadn't liked, for you never know what people will think. He was not forgetting that there was an Englishman in the house.

"It's about Marcellin," she went on to say, blushing. "He talked to me one afternoon when he was very drunk and took his siesta on the café bench."

Well! Not so long ago, too, when the Arche was empty, he had seen someone stretched out on that same bench, a newspaper over his face, taking a short nap. It was evidently a cool spot. An odd house, even so! As for the smell . . .

"I thought it might be of some use to you. He told me that, if he wanted, he could have a pile as big as that."

"A pile of what?"

"Of banknotes, of course."

"A long time ago?"

"I think it was two days before what happened."

"There wasn't anyone else in the café?"

"I was alone, polishing the counter."

"Did you tell anyone about it?"

"I don't think so."

"He didn't say anything else?"

"Only: '*What would I do with it, my little Jojo? It's so nice here.*'"

"He never made love to you, never made any proposals?"

"No."

"And the others?"

"Nearly all of them."

"When Ginette was here—she came almost every month, didn't she?—did Marcellin ever happen to go up to see her in her bedroom?"

"Certainly not. He was very respectful toward her."

"Can I speak to you like a grown-up, Jojo?"

"I'm nineteen, you know."

"Good. Did Marcellin have relations with women, now and again?"

"Certainly."

"On the island?"

"With Nine, to start with. That's my cousin. She does it with everybody. It seems she can't help it."

"On board his boat?"

"Anywhere. Then with the widow Lambert, who keeps the café on the other side of the square. He would sometimes spend the night with her. Whenever he caught some sea wolves, he would bring them to her. I suppose, now he's dead, I can tell you: Marcellin fished with dynamite."

"There was never any question of his marrying the widow Lambert?"

"I don't think she wants to remarry."

And Jojo's smile let it be understood that the widow Lambert was no ordinary person.

"Is that all, Jojo?"

"Yes. I'd better be going down again."

Ginette wasn't asleep either. She lay in the next room, just behind the partition, so that Maigret had the impression that he could hear her breathing. It made him feel uncomfortable because when he turned over, half-asleep, he sometimes banged the partition with his elbow and each time that must have made her jump.

It had been a very long time before she went off to sleep. What could she have been doing? Seeing to her face or her toilet? The silence at times was so profound in her bedroom that Maigret wondered if she was in the middle of writing something. Especially as the attic window was too high for her to be able to lean out and breathe the fresh air.

That famous smell again . . . It was, quite simply, the smell of Porquerolles. He had caught it at the end of the jetty, a short while ago, with Mr. Pyke. There were whiffs of smells from the water, overheated by the sun during the day, and others coming from the land with the breeze. Weren't the trees in the square eucalyptus? There were probably other natural scents on the island.

Who was it going down the passage again? Mr. Pyke? It was the third time. Paul's cooking, for which he was so ill acclimatized, must have upset him.

He had drunk a lot, had Mr. Pyke. Was it from choice, or because he had been unable to do otherwise? At all events he liked champagne and Maigret had never thought of offering him any. He had drunk it all evening with the major. They got on so well together from the start, that one might have thought they had always known one another. They had settled themselves in a corner. On instructions, Jojo had brought champagne.

Bellam didn't drink it in champagne glasses, but in large ones, like beer glasses. He was so perfect that he looked like a drawing in *Punch*, with his silvery gray hair, his rosy complexion, large clear eyes swimming in liquid, and the huge cigar which never left his lips.

He was an old boy of seventy or seventy-two years, with a mischievous twinkle in his eye. His voice, probably because of the champagne and the cigars, was husky. Even after several bottles, he maintained an affecting dignity.

"May I introduce Major Bellam?" Mr. Pyke had said at a certain moment. "It turns out we were at the same school."

Not the same year, at all events, nor the same decade. One could feel that this gave them both pleasure. The major called the chief inspector "Monsieur Maigrette."

From time to time he would give an almost imperceptible signal to Jojo or Paul, which was enough for them to bring fresh champagne to the table. At other times, a different sign would bring Jojo, who would pour out a glass and take it over to someone in the room.

This might have had something haughty or condescending about it. The major did it so charmingly, so naively, that it gave no offense. He looked a little as if he were distributing good marks. When the glass had arrived at its destination, he raised his own and drank a silent toast from where he sat.

Everyone, or almost everyone, dropped in. Charlot, almost the whole evening, had been working the crane. He had started off by playing with the fruit machine and he could allow himself to spend as much as he liked since it was he who collected the kitty. The crane must have belonged to him as well. He fitted a coin into the slot, and with sustained concentration turned the knob, directing the small chromium pincers toward a cheap cigarette case, or a pipe, or a wallet from a bazaar.

Was Ginette not sleeping because she was worried? Had Maigret been too harsh with her? In the bedroom, yes, he had been hard. It was not out of spite, as might have been thought. Had she thought it was out of spite?

It is always ridiculous to play the Good Samaritan. He had picked her up in the Place des Ternes and had sent her off to the sanatorium. He had never told himself he was saving a soul, that he was "snatching a girl from the gutter."

Someone else, "who was like him," as she had told him, had looked after her in his turn: the doctor at the sanatorium. Had he been hoping for something?

She had become what she had become. That was her affair. He had no reason to take offense, to resent it with bitterness.

He had been hard because it had been a necessity, because that type of woman, even the least wicked of them, lie as they breathe, sometimes without any need, without any reason. And she hadn't told him everything yet, he was sure. So much so that she couldn't get to sleep. There was something on her mind.

Once, she got up. He heard her bare feet on the floor of the room. Was she going to come and find him? There was nothing impossible about that, and Maigret had prepared himself mentally to hurry into his trousers, which he had left lying on the floor.

She hadn't come. There had been the clink of a glass. She was thirsty. Or else she had taken a sleeping pill.

He had only drunk one glass of champagne. The rest of the time he had drunk mostly wine, then, God knows why, anisette.

Who had ordered anisette? Oh yes, it was the dentist. A retired dentist, to be precise, whose name escaped him. Another phenomenon. There were nothing but phenomena on the island, at the Arche at any rate. Or perhaps was it they who were right and the people on the other side of the water, on the mainland, who were wrong to behave otherwise?

He must once have been very respectable, very well groomed, for he had a dentist's surgery in one of the smartest districts of Bordeaux, and the people of Bordeaux are particular. He had come to Porquerolles by chance, on holiday, and since then he had only left for a week, the time it took to go and wind up his affairs.

He wore no collar. It was one of the Morins, a fisherman, who cut his hair once a month. That Morin was called Morin-Coiffeur. The ex-dentist's beard was at least three days old and he neglected his hands, he neglected everything, didn't do anything, except read, in a rocking chair, in the shade on his veranda.

He had married a girl on the island who had perhaps been pretty but who had very quickly become enormous, with the shadow of a mustache on her lip and a strident voice.

He was happy. Or so he claimed. He would say with a disconcerting assurance:

"You'll see! If you stay long enough, you'll be bitten, like the others. And then you won't go away again."

Maigret knew that, on certain of the Pacific islands, white people sometimes let themselves go like that, go native, as they say, but he didn't know it was possible three miles from the French coast.

When someone was mentioned to the dentist, he only judged them in terms of the extent to which they had gone native. He called it something else. He said: Porquerollitis.

The doctor? For there was a doctor, too, whom Maigret had not yet met, but Lechat had mentioned him. Infected to the bone, according to the dentist.

"I presume you are friends?"

"We never see one another. We pass the time of day, at a distance."

True, the doctor had arrived with his preoccupations. He was very ill and had only settled in the island to cure himself. He was a bachelor. He lived alone in a poky little house with a garden full of flowers and he did his own housework. Indoors, it was very dirty. On account of his health, he didn't go out in the evenings, even in cases of emergency, and, in winter, if it happened to be really cold, which was rare, days and sometimes weeks would go by without his white nose being seen.

"You'll see! You'll see!" the dentist insisted with a sarcastic smile. "Besides, you've already got some idea of what it is by looking around you. Just think, it's the same every evening."

And it was indeed a curious spectacle. It wasn't quite the atmosphere of a café, nor was it that of a drawing room. The disorder called to mind a soirée in an artist's studio.

Everyone knew everyone else and people didn't stand on ceremony for each other. The major, who came from a leading English school, was here on the same footing as a dockside loafer like Marcellin, or as a Charlot.

From time to time, someone would change places, or partners.

To start with, Monsieur Émile and Ginette had remained still and quiet at the same table, near the counter, like a long-married couple waiting for a train in a railway station. Monsieur Émile had ordered his usual tisane, Ginette a greenish liqueur in a minute glass.

Now and then they would exchange a word or two, in a low voice. Nothing could be heard. Only the movement of their lips could be seen. Then Ginette had risen with a sigh and gone off to fetch a game of checkers from a cabinet under the gramophone.

They played. One felt that it might have been like that every day, for years on end, that the people would grow old without changing their places, without attempting any actions other than the ones they were to be seen making now.

No doubt in five years Maigret would find the dentist in front of the same anisette, with an identical smile, at once savage and satisfied. Charlot was working the crane with the movements of an automaton, and there was no reason for that to stop at a given moment.

The engaged couple moved the men about on the checkerboard, which they contemplated with unreal gravity between each move, and the major emptied glass after glass of champagne, while he recounted stories to Mr. Pyke.

No one was in a hurry. No one seemed to think that tomorrow existed. When she hadn't any customer to serve, Jojo went and leaned on the counter and, with her chin on her hand, gazed thoughtfully in front of her.

Several times Maigret felt her eyes fixed on him, but the moment he turned his head she would look away.

Paul, the *patron*, still in his cook's attire, went from table to table, and at each he offered a round of drinks. It must have cost him a lot, but it is to be presumed that he made it up in the long run.

As for his wife, a small person with faded blonde hair, hard-faced, who was scarcely noticed, she had settled down by herself at a table and was doing the day's accounts.

"It's like this every evening," Lechat had told the chief inspector.

"And the islanders, the fishermen I mean?"

"They hardly ever come after dinner. They go out to sea before daybreak and retire early to bed. At any rate, in the evening, they wouldn't come to the Arche. It's a sort of tacit agreement. In the afternoon, the morning as well, everyone mixes. After dinner, the islanders, the real inhabitants, prefer to go to the other cafés."

"What do they do?"

"Nothing. I've been to see them. Sometimes they listen to the wireless, but that's fairly unusual. They have a small drink in silence, staring in front of them."

"Is it always as calm here?"

"It all depends. Listen. It can happen from one moment to another. It takes a mere nothing, a remark in the air, a round of drinks offered by one person or another, and everyone groups together, and starts talking at once."

It hadn't happened, perhaps because of the presence of Maigret.

It was hot, in spite of the open window. It had become an obsession to listen to the noises of the house. Ginette was still not asleep. There were occasional footsteps above his head. As for Mr. Pyke, he had to go a fourth time to the end of the passage and, each time, Maigret waited with a sort of anguish for the racket caused by the flush, before attempting to go back to sleep. For he must have been sleeping between the interruptions, a sleep not deep enough to efface his thoughts completely, but sufficient to distort them.

Mr. Pyke had played a dirty trick on him when he had spoken about the Dutchman at the end of the jetty. From now on the chief inspector could only see de Greef in the light of the peremptory phrases of his British colleague.

However, the portrait which Pyke had sketched of the young man did not satisfy him. He, too, was there, with Anna, who must have been sleepy and who, as time passed, allowed herself to lean more and more on her companion's shoulder.

De Greef did not speak to her. He cannot have been in the habit of speaking to her often. He was the male, the leader, and she had only to follow, to await his pleasure.

He was watching. With his very thin face he called to mind a lean animal, a wild beast.

The others probably weren't lambs, but indisputably de Greef was a wild beast. He sniffed like a wild beast. It was a mannerism. He would listen to what was being said and then he would sniff. That was his only perceptible reaction.

In the jungle the major would probably have been a pachyderm, an elephant, or better still a hippopotamus. And Monsieur Émile? Something furtive, with pointed teeth.

It was absurd. What would Mr. Pyke have thought if he had been able to read Maigret's thoughts? True, the chief inspector had the excuse of having had too much to drink and being half-asleep. If he had foreseen his insomnia he would have accounted for a few more glasses, in order to plunge at once into a dreamless slumber.

All in all Lechat was a very good man. So good that Maigret would have liked to have had him in his service. Still a little young, a little excitable. He was easily agitated, like a gun dog which runs in all directions around its master.

He knew the Midi already, as he had been in the squad at Draguignan, but he had only had occasion to visit Porquerolles once or twice; he had only really got to know the island during the last two or three days.

"The people from the *North Star* don't come every evening?"

"Almost every evening. They sometimes arrive late. Usually, when the sea is calm, they come by moonlight in a dinghy."

"Are Mrs. Wilcox and the major friends?"

"They studiously avoid speaking to one another, and each looks at the other as though they didn't exist."

After all, it was understandable. They both had the same background. Both, for one reason or another, had come here to let their hair down.

The major must have been very embarrassed becoming drunk under the eye of Mrs. Wilcox, for in his country, gentlemen do that among themselves, behind closed doors.

As for her, in front of the retired Indian Army officer, she cannot have been very proud of her Moricourt.

They had arrived about eleven o'clock in the evening. As nearly always happens, she was nothing like the idea the chief inspector had formed of her in his mind.

He had imagined a lady, and she was a redhead—of an artificial red—rather a stout woman on the wane, whose broken voice recalled that of Major Bellam, only it was louder. She was wearing a linen dress, but she had round her neck three strings of pearls which were perhaps genuine, and a large diamond on her finger.

Straightaway she had singled out Maigret. Philippe must have told her about the chief inspector and from the moment she sat down she hadn't ceased sizing him up and discussing him in a low voice with her companion.

What was she saying? Did she, on her side, find him heavy and vulgar? Had she pictured him as a film star? Perhaps she thought he didn't look very intelligent?

The two of them were drinking whisky, with very little soda. Philippe waited on her hand and foot and the chief inspector's attention irritated him; he evidently didn't like being seen in the exercise of his functions. As for her, she was doing it on purpose. Instead of summoning Jojo or Paul, she would send her beau to change her glass, which she didn't find clean enough, or made him get up again to go and fetch her some cigarettes from the counter. Another time, God knows why, she sent him outside.

She had to assert her power over the heir of the Moricourts, and perhaps, by the same token, to show that she was unashamed.

As they passed, the couple had greeted the young de Greef and his companion. Very vaguely. Rather in the way that masonic signs are exchanged.

The major, contrary to Maigret's expectations, had been the first to leave, dignified but uncertain in his bearing, and Mr. Pyke had gone some of the way with him.

Then the dentist, in his turn, had left.

"You'll see. You'll see!" he had repeated to Maigret, as he predicted for him a speedy onset of Porquerollitis.

Charlot, who had had enough of the crane, had gone to sit jockey-style on a chair, next to the checkers game, and, silently, had pointed out one or two moves to Ginette. Once Monsieur Émile had left, he had gone up to bed. As for Ginette, she seemed to be waiting for Maigret's permission. In the end she had come over to his table and murmured, with a little smile:

"Still cross with me?"

She was visibly tired, and he had advised her to go up to bed. He had gone up straightaway after her, because the idea had come to him that she might be going to join Charlot.

At one moment, when he was trying to go to sleep—but perhaps he was already asleep and it was only a dream?—he had had the impression that he had discovered a really important fact.

"I mustn't forget it. It is essential that I should remember it tomorrow morning."

He had all but got up and made a note of it on a piece of paper. It had come to him in a flash. It was very odd. He was pleased. He kept repeating to himself:

"Above all, I mustn't forget it in the morning!"

And the flushing of the lavatory once more set the Arche resounding with its racket. Afterwards there were ten minutes of listening to the water slowly flowing back into the cistern. It was exasperating. The noise was becoming louder. There were explosions. Maigret sat up in bed, opened his eyes, and found the room bathed in sunlight, with, just in front of him, framed in the open window, the belfry of the little church.

The explosions were coming from the port. It was the engines of the boats being started up, and coughing. All the fishermen were leaving at the same time. One of the motors kept on stopping after several efforts, and a silence followed, then again the coughing sound, so that one wanted to go and help to get it going properly once and for all.

He felt like getting dressed and going out of doors, then looked at the time by his watch, which he had put on the bedside table, and found it was only half-past four in the morning. The smell was still more pronounced than on the day before, probably because of the damp of the dawn. There was no sound in the house, no sound in the square, where the foliage of the eucalyptus trees was motionless in the rising sun. Only the motors, in the harbor, an occasional voice, then even the thrumming of the motors died away in the distance, and, for a very long time, was no more than a vibration in the air.

When he opened his eyes once more, another smell reminded him of all the mornings since his early childhood, the smell of fresh coffee, and from most parts of the house came the buzz of activity, footsteps could be heard on the square, brooms frisking against the stones in the roadway.

He was at once aware that there was something of vital importance that he had to remember, but could bring back to mind no distinct memory. His mouth was lined with fur, because of the anisette. He felt for a bell button in the hope of having some coffee sent up. There was none. Then he put on his trousers, his shirt, his slippers, ran a comb through his hair and opened his door. A strong smell of scent and soap was issuing from Ginette's room, where she must have been busy at her toilet.

Wasn't it about her that he had made, or thought he had made, a discovery? He went down and, in the main room, found the chairs in pyramids on the tables. The doors were open and the chairs on the terrace were similarly stacked up. There was nobody about.

He went into the kitchen, which seemed dark to him, had to accustom his eyes to the half-light.

"Good morning, chief inspector. Did you sleep well?"

It was Jojo, with her black dress, which was too short and literally clung to her body. She hadn't yet washed either, and she seemed to be naked underneath.

"Will you have some coffee?"

For a second he thought of Madame Maigret who at that hour would be preparing the breakfast in their flat in Paris, with the windows open on to the Boulevard Richard-Lenoir. It struck him that it was raining in Paris. When he had left it was almost as cold as in winter. From here it seemed incredible.

"Shall I clear a table for you?"

What for? He was perfectly all right in the kitchen. She was cooking some vine stalks on the kitchen stove, and it smelled good. When she lifted her arms he could see the small brown hairs of her armpits.

He was still searching his mind for the discovery of the night before, uttering words without thinking, perhaps because he was embarrassed to be alone with Jojo.

"Isn't Monsieur Paul up yet?"

"He's already been at the harbor a good while. He goes every morning to buy his fish from the boats as they come back."

She glanced at the clock.

"The *Cormorant* leaves in five minutes."

"Is anyone else up?"

"Monsieur Charlot."

"Not with his luggage, I presume?"

"No. He's with Monsieur Paul. Your friend has gone out too, at least a quarter of an hour ago."

Maigret contemplated the expanse of the square through the open windows.

"He's probably in the water. He was wearing a bathing suit, with his towel under his arm."

It had something to do with Ginette. But it was also linked in his mind with Jojo. He remembered that, in his half-sleep, he had recalled Jojo at the moment she was going up the stairs. Now this wasn't an erotic thought. The legs she disclosed were only incidental to it. Let's see! Later on, she had come into his room.

The day before, he had persistently asked Ginette:

"Why have you come?"

And she had lied several times. At first she had said that it was to see him, because she had learned that he was on the island and had assumed he would send for her.

A little later, she was admitting that she was in a sort of way engaged to Monsieur Émile. This meant admitting at the same time that she had come to clear him, to assure the chief inspector that her employer was in no way concerned with Marcellin's death.

He hadn't been so very wrong to be hard with her. She had yielded some ground. But she hadn't yet yielded enough.

He was drinking his coffee in small sips, standing in front of the stove. By a curious coincidence, the cup of common china, but of an old-fashioned design, was almost a replica of the one he used during his childhood, which he then imagined to be unique.

"Aren't you having anything to eat?"

"Not now."

"In a quarter of an hour, there will be fresh bread at the baker's."

In the end he relaxed, and Jojo must have wondered why he began to smile. He had remembered.

Hadn't Marcellin mentioned to Jojo a "packet" which he could have had? He was drunk, certainly, but he often was drunk. For how long had the possibility of laying his hands on this "packet" been here? It wasn't necessarily recent. Ginette used to visit the island practically every month. She had come the month before. It was easy to check into. Marcellin, on the other hand, could have written to her.

If he was able to get hold of a packet, it was probable that someone else could get it in his place, for instance by knowing what he knew.

Maigret stayed where he was, cup in hand, staring at the brightly lit rectangle of the door and Jojo kept darting curious glances at him.

Lechat claimed that Marcel died because he had talked too much about "his friend Maigret" and, at first sight, this appeared to make sense.

It was odd to see Mr. Pyke, almost naked, come out into the light, his soaked towel in his hand, his hair stuck to his forehead.

Instead of greeting him, Maigret murmured:

"Just a moment . . ."

He almost had it. A slight effort and his idea would fall into place. Starting off, for example, with the notion that Ginette had come because she knew why Marcellin had died.

She hadn't necessarily put herself out to prevent the discovery of the guilty party. Once she had married Monsieur Émile she would be rich, certainly. Only old Justine wasn't dead yet, she might linger on for years, despite the doctors. If she discovered what was afoot, she was quite capable of playing a dirty trick so as to prevent her son marrying anyone after her death.

Marcellin's "packet" was to be had straightaway. Perhaps it was still there to be got? In spite of the presence of Maigret and the Inspector Lechat?

"I beg your pardon, Mr. Pyke. Did you sleep well?"

"Very well," replied the Englishman imperturbably.

Was Maigret to admit that he had counted the times the lavatory was flushed? It was not necessary and, after his bath, the Scotland Yard inspector was as fresh as a fish.

Presently, while he was shaving, the chief inspector would have time to think about the "packet."

6

There is something to be said for the English. Would a French colleague, in Mr. Pyke's place, have been able to resist the desire to score a point? And hadn't Maigret, who was not especially given to teasing, all but made a discreet allusion, just now, to the lavatory which the Yard inspector had flushed so many times during the night?

Perhaps more alcohol had flowed that evening than either of them had imagined? At all events it was rather unexpected. There were still the three of them, Maigret, Pyke, and Jojo, in the kitchen with the door left open. Maigret was finishing his coffee, and Mr. Pyke, in his bathing trunks, was standing between him and the light, while Jojo was trying to find some bacon for him in the larder. It was exactly three minutes to eight and then, looking at the clock, Maigret declared in that innocent, inimitable voice that comes to one in moments of gaffes:

"I wonder if Lechat is still sleeping off his wine from last night."

Jojo started, but managed not to turn round. As for Mr. Pyke, all his good education failed to prevent the round look of astonishment being seen to light up his face. It was, however, with perfect simplicity that he uttered:

"I've just seen him taking his place on board the *Cormorant*. I presume it will wait for Ginette."

Maigret had done nothing more or less than forget all about Marcellin's funeral. Worse still, it suddenly came back to him that the day before he had talked about it for a long time, with even a little too much insistence, to the inspector. Was Mr. Pyke present at that conversation? He couldn't have said, but he could picture himself again, seated on the bench.

"You go with her, old man, you get the idea? I don't say it'll lead anywhere. Perhaps she will show some reaction, perhaps not. Perhaps someone will try to speak to her on the sly. Perhaps recognizing a face in the congregation may tell you something. One should always go to funerals, it's an old principle that has often succeeded. Keep your eyes open. That's all."

He seemed even to recall that, while chatting away to the inspector, he had related one or two stories of funerals which had put him on the track of criminals.

He understood now why Ginette had made so much noise in her bedroom. He heard her opening her door and calling out from upstairs:

"Pour me out a cup of coffee, Jojo. How much time have I got?"

"Three minutes, madame!"

Just at that moment, the sound of a siren was announcing the *Cormorant*'s imminent departure.

"I'll come as far as the landing stage," the chief inspector announced.

In his slippers and with no collar, for he hadn't time to go up and get dressed. He wasn't the only one in that attire. There were little groups in the neighborhood of the boat, still the same ones as had been there the day before when the chief inspector had landed. They must have attended all the departures and all the arrivals. Before starting the day they would come to watch the *Cormorant* leaving the harbor, after which, delaying their morning toilet a little longer, they would have a glass of white wine at Paul's or in one of the cafés.

The dentist, less discreet than Mr. Pyke, looked hard at Maigret's slippers and his state of undress, and his satisfied smile was saying unambiguously:

"I warned you! It's started!"

Porquerollitis, presumably, in which he himself was steeped to the marrow. Aloud, he contented himself with asking:

"Slept well?"

Lechat, already on board, petulant, impatient, went ashore again to have a word with his chief.

"I didn't want to wake you up. Isn't she coming? Baptiste says that if she doesn't come at once, they'll go off without her."

There were others making the crossing for Marcellin's funeral, fishermen in their Sunday best, the builder, the tobacconist. Maigret couldn't see Charlot around and yet he had spotted him just now in the square. Nothing was moving aboard the *North Star*. At the moment the dumb sailor was about to cast off, Ginette appeared, half-walking, half-running, dressed in black silk with a black hat and a veil, leaving a rustling and scented wake behind her. She was whisked on board as though by a conjuring trick, and it was not until she was seated that she saw the chief inspector on the jetty and wished him good morning with a little nod of her head.

The sea was so smooth, so luminous, that when one stared at it for long one could no longer distinguish, for a moment or two, the shape of things. The *Cormorant* described a silver curve on the water. The people waited another moment watching her, from habit and tradition, then set off, slowly, toward the square. A fisherman, who had just spiked an octopus with his harpoon, was skinning it and the tentacles were coiling round his tattooed arm.

At the Arche, Paul, bright-eyed, was serving out white wine from behind his counter, and Mr. Pyke, who had had time to dress, was at a table eating bacon and eggs. Maigret drank a glass of wine, like the others, and a little later, while he was busy shaving in front of his window, with his braces hanging over his thighs, there was a knock at the door.

It was the Englishman.

"Am I in the way? May I come in?"

He sat in the only chair, and the silence was a long one.

"I spent part of the evening chatting with the major," he said finally. "Do you know he was one of our best polo players?"

He must have been disappointed with the reaction, or to be more precise, with the lack of reaction on the part of Maigret. The latter had only a vague notion of the game of polo. All he knew was that it was played from horseback and that somewhere, in the Bois de Boulogne or at St. Cloud, there was a very aristocratic polo club.

Mr. Pyke, with a guileless air, stretched out a helping hand.

"He's a younger son."

For him, this meant a lot. In England, in great families, isn't it the eldest son alone who inherits title and fortune, which obliges the others to make a career for themselves in the army or the navy?

"His brother is a member of the House of Lords. The major chose the Indian Army."

The same phenomenon must take place, in reverse, when Maigret made allusions to his English colleague about people like Charlot, or Monsieur Émile, or Ginette. But Mr. Pyke was being patient, dotting his i's with an exquisite discretion, almost without touching them.

"People with a certain name are reluctant to remain in London unless they have the means to cut a fine figure there. The great passion in the Indian Army is horses. To play polo a stable of several ponies is essential."

"The major's never got married?"

"Younger sons seldom marry. In taking charge of a family Bellam would have had to give up his horses."

"And he preferred the horses!"

This did not seem at all surprising to Mr. Pyke.

"In the evening, out there, the bachelors gather at the club and have no distraction besides drink. The major has drunk a lot in his time. In India it was whisky. It was only here that he took to champagne."

"Did he tell you why he chose to live in Porquerolles?"

"He had an appalling tragedy, the worst that could have befallen him. As a result of a bad fall from his horse, he was immobilized in bed for three years, half of the time in a cast and, when he was on his feet again, he realized that his riding days were over."

"That's the reason he left India?"

"That's why he's here. I'm sure that almost everywhere in climates like this, in the Mediterranean or the Pacific, you will find old gentlemen of the same type as the major, who are considered eccentrics. Where else could they go?"

"Don't they have any desire to go back to England?"

"Their means won't permit them to live in London according to their rank, and the habits they have adopted would be frowned upon in the country in England."

"Did he tell you why he doesn't speak to Mrs. Wilcox?"

"There was no need for him to tell me."

Should he persist? Or would Mr. Pyke, too, prefer not to hear too much about his compatriot? Mrs. Wilcox, to put it in a nutshell, was not as a woman what the major was as a man.

Maigret wiped his cheeks, hesitated about putting on his jacket. The Yard inspector had not put on his. It was already hot. But the chief inspector could not allow himself, like his slim colleague, not to wear braces, and a man in braces always looks like a shopkeeper on a picnic.

He put his jacket on. They had nothing else to do in the room, and Mr. Pyke murmured as he rose:

"The major, despite everything, has remained a gentleman."

He followed Maigret down the stairs. He didn't ask what he intended to do, but he was following him, and that was enough to spoil the chief inspector's day.

He had vaguely promised himself, expressly on Mr. Pyke's account, to behave that morning like a high police official. In theory, a Police Headquarters chief inspector does not run around streets and bars looking for murderers. He is an important man, who spends most of his time in his office, and like a general in his HQ, directs a small army of sergeants, inspectors, and technicians.

Maigret had never been able to resign himself to this. Like a gun dog, he had to ferret things out for himself, to scratch and sniff the smells.

The first two days, Lechat had got through a considerable amount of work and had handed over to Maigret an account of all the interrogations he had carried out.

The whole island had been put through it, the Morins and the Gallis, the sick doctor, the priest, whom Maigret hadn't yet seen, and the women as well.

Maigret would have installed himself in a corner of the dining room, which was empty all the morning, and he would have zealously studied these reports, marking them with a blue or red pencil.

With an uneasy glance, he asked Mr. Pyke:

"Does it happen at the Yard for your colleagues to run about the streets like novices?"

"I know at least three or four who are never to be seen in their offices."

So much the better, for he had no desire to remain sitting down. He was beginning to understand why the people of Porquerolles were always to be found in the same places. It was instinctive. Despite oneself one was to some extent affected by the sun, by the landscape. Now, for example, Maigret and his companion were taking a walk out of doors, without any definite direction, and hardly noticing that they were going down toward the harbor.

Maigret was sure that if, by chance, he was obliged to spend the rest of his days on the island, he would take the same walk every morning and that the pipe he smoked then would always be the best pipe of the day. The *Cormorant*, over there, on the other side of the water, at Giens Point, was disgorging its passengers, who were piling into an old bus. Even with the naked eye one could make out the boat as a tiny white dot.

The mute would be about to load up some crates of vegetables and fruit for the mayor and for the Cooperative, meat for the butcher, and the mailbags. People would embark perhaps, as Maigret and Mr. Pyke had embarked the day before, and would no doubt experience the same feeling of vertigo on discovering the underwater landscape.

The sailors on the big white yacht were washing down the deck. They were middle-aged men who from time to time went for a drink, without mixing with the locals, at Morin-Barbu's.

To the right of the harbor a footpath ran up the steep slope, like a cliff, and ended at a hut, with the door open.

A fisherman, sitting in the doorway, was holding a net stretched out between his bare toes, and his hands, as nimble as a seamstress's, were passing a netting hook in and out of the holes.

It was here that Marcellin had been killed. The two policemen glanced at the interior. The center was occupied by a huge cauldron, like the ones used in the country for boiling pig swill. Here it was the nets that were put to boil in a brown mixture which protected them against the action of the sea water.

Marcellin must have used old sails as a mattress, and in the corners there were pots of paint scattered about, oil or kerosene cans, pieces of scrap iron, patched-up oars.

"Do other people ever sleep here?" Maigret asked the fisherman.

The latter raised his head indifferently.

"Old Benoît, sometimes, when it's raining."

"And when it's not raining?"

"He prefers to sleep out of doors. It depends. Sometimes it's in a cove or on the deck of a boat. Sometimes on a bench in the square."

"Have you seen him today?"

"He was over there just now."

The fisherman pointed at the footpath which continued beside the sea at a certain height and which, on one side, was bordered with pine trees.

"Was he alone?"

"I think the gentleman from the Arche joined up with him a little further on."

"Which one?"

"The one with a linen suit and a white cap."

It was Charlot.

"Did he come back this way?"

"A good half hour ago."

The *Cormorant* was still no more than a white dot in the blue of the world, but the white dot, now, was clearly separated from the shore. Other boats were dotted about on the sea, some motionless, some progressing slowly, leaving a luminous wake behind them.

Maigret and Mr. Pyke went down to the harbor once more, followed along the jetty, as on the previous evening, mechanically watched a boy fishing for conger eels with a short line.

When they passed in front of the Dutchman's little boat, Maigret glanced inside and was somewhat surprised to see Charlot in conversation with de Greef.

Mr. Pyke was still following him, silently. Was he expecting something to happen? Was he trying to guess Maigret's thoughts?

They went to the end of the pier, retraced their steps, came once more past the *Fleur d'amour*, and Charlot was still in the same place.

Three times they covered the hundred yards of the pier, and the third time Charlot climbed onto the deck of the little yacht, turned around to say good-bye and stepped onto the plank which served as a gangway.

The two men were just near to him. They were going to pass one another. Maigret, after hesitating, stopped. It was the time when the bus from Giens should be arriving at Hyères. The people for the funeral would go and have a drink before heading for the morgue.

"I say, I was looking for you this morning."

"As you can see, I didn't leave the island."

"That's just what I wanted to talk to you about. I see no reason for keeping you here any longer. You told me, I think, that you had only come for two or three days and that, but for Marcellin's death, you would have left by now. The inspector thought it right to make you stay. I'll set you free again."

"Thank you."

"I only ask that you tell me where I can find you in case I need you."

Charlot, who was smoking, studied the end of his cigarette for a moment as though reflecting.

"At the Arche!" he finally said.

"You aren't going away then?"

"Not for the moment."

And, lifting his head again, he looked the chief inspector in the eye.

"Does that surprise you? One might think you were annoyed to see me stay. I suppose it's allowed?"

"I can't stop you. I admit I should be curious to know what made you change your mind."

"I haven't got a particularly absorbing profession, have I? No office or factory or business premises, no employees or workers waiting for me. Don't you find it pleasant here?"

He made no attempt to conceal his irony. They could see the mayor, still in his long gray smock, coming down toward the harbor pushing his wheelbarrow. The page from the Grand Hôtel was there as well, and the porter with the uniform cap.

The *Cormorant* was now just midway in the crossing and would reach the disembarkation point in a quarter of an hour.

"You've had a long conversation with old Benoît?"

"When I saw you just now near the hut, I thought you would ask me that. You'll question Benoît in your turn. I can't stop you, but I can tell you in advance that he knows nothing. At any rate, that's what I gathered, for it's not easy to interpret his language. Perhaps, after all, you'll be luckier than I was."

"You are trying to find out something?"

"Perhaps the same thing as you."

It was a challenge almost, thrown out with good humor.

"What makes you think it could be of interest to you? Did Marcellin talk to you?"

"No more than to the others. He was always a little embarrassed in front of me. The half-and-halfs are never at their ease in front of the *caïds*."

Presently the word *caïd* would have to be explained to Mr. Pyke, who was visibly setting it to one side in a compartment of his brain.

Maigret joined in the game, spoke also in an undertone, lightly, as though uttering words of no consequence.

"You know why Marcellin was killed, Charlot?"

"I know almost as much as you. And, indeed, I probably draw the same conclusions, but with different ends."

He smiled, crinkling up his eyelids in the sun.

"Has Jojo talked to you?"

"To me? Haven't you been told that we hate one another like cat and dog?"

"Have you done something to her?"

"She didn't want me to. That's just what's kept us apart."

"I wonder, Charlot, if you wouldn't do better to return to Pont du Las."

"And I, with all due respect for your advice, prefer to remain."

A dinghy was detaching itself from the *North Star*, and on it Moricourt's silhouette could be recognized as he sat at the oars. He was the only person aboard. Like the others, he was doubtless coming over for the arrival of the *Cormorant*, and would go up as far as the post office to collect his mail.

Charlot, following Maigret's gaze, seemed at the same time to be following his thoughts. As the chief inspector had turned toward the Dutchman's boat, he declared:

"He's a strange fellow, but I don't think it's him."

"You mean Marcellin's murderer?"

"One can hide nothing from you. Mark you, the murderer doesn't interest me in himself. Only, except in the course of a fit, one doesn't kill someone without any reason, does one? Even and above all if that someone proclaims to whoever wants to hear that he's a friend of Chief Inspector Maigret."

"You were at the Arche when Marcellin mentioned me?"

"Everyone was there. I mean, all the people you are busying yourself with. And Marcellin, especially after a few drinks, had a pretty piercing voice."

"Do you know why he said that, on that particular evening?"

"There you are. As you may imagine that was the first question I asked myself when I learned that he was dead, I wondered who the poor fellow was speaking to. Do you understand?"

Maigret understood perfectly.

"Did you find a satisfactory reply?"

"Not so far. If I had found one, I should have returned to Pont du Las by the next boat."

"I didn't know you liked playing amateur detectives."

"You're joking, inspector."

The latter still persisted, with an air of utter indifference, in trying to make the other say something he was refusing to say.

It was a strange sort of game, in the sun on the jetty, with Mr. Pyke playing the part of umpire and remaining strictly neutral.

"So you definitely start from the idea that Marcellin was not killed without good reason?"

"As you say."

"You suppose the murderer was trying to appropriate something which Marcellin had in his possession."

"Neither you nor I suppose anything of the sort, or else your reputation is damned overrated."

"Someone wanted to shut his mouth?"

"You're getting very warm, inspector."

"He had made a discovery which could endanger someone?"

"Why are you so anxious to know what I think when all the time you know as much about it as I do?"

"Including the 'big money'?"

"Including the 'big money.'"

After which, lighting a fresh cigar, Charlot threw out:

"Big money has always interested me; do you catch on now?"

"That's why you visited the Dutchman this morning?"

"He's flat broke."

"Which means it's not him?"

"I don't say that. All I say is that Marcellin couldn't have hoped to get money out of him."

"You're forgetting the girl."

"Anna?"

"Her father is very rich."

That made Charlot think, but he finally shrugged his shoulders. The *Cormorant* was passing by the first rocky promontory and entering the harbor.

"Will you excuse me? I'm probably meeting someone."

And Charlot touched his cap ironically, and headed for the jetty.

While Maigret was stuffing his pipe, Mr. Pyke declared:

"I think he's a highly intelligent fellow."

"It's pretty hard to succeed in his job without being."

The page boy from the Grand Hôtel was taking the luggage of a young married couple. The mayor, who had gone aboard, was examining the labels on the packages. Charlot was helping a young woman ashore, and was taking her toward the Arche. So he really was waiting for someone. He must have telephoned the day before.

As a matter of fact, where had Inspector Lechat telephoned Maigret from, two days before, to tell him about it all? If it was from the Arche, where the wall telephone was just beside the bar, everyone had overheard him. He must remember to ask him.

The dentist was there again, in the same clothes as in the morning, unshaven, perhaps unwashed, an old straw hat on his head. He was watching the *Cormorant*, and that was enough for him. He seemed happy to be alive.

Were Maigret and Mr. Pyke to follow the general movement, stroll up to the Arche, make for the bar, and drink the white wine which would be served up without their being asked what they wanted?

The chief inspector studied his companion from the corner of his eye, and on his side Mr. Pyke, though impassive, seemed to be studying him.

Why not follow the others, after all? Marcellin's burial was in progress at Hyères. Behind the bier Ginette was taking the place of the family and she would be mopping her brow with her handkerchief, screwed tightly into a ball. There was a heavy heat in the air over there, in the avenues lined with motionless palms.

"Do you like the island white wine, Monsieur Pyke?"

"I should be very happy to drink a glass."

The postman was crossing the bare expanse of the square pushing a barrow piled with the mailbags. Lifting his head, Maigret saw the windows of the Arche wide open and, in one of the frames on the first floor, Charlot leaning on the window sill. Behind him in the gilded half-light, a young woman was in the act of removing her dress, which she was slipping over her head.

"He talked a lot and I wonder if he was hoping to get more out of me."

That would emerge later. People like Charlot cannot easily resist adopting an advantageous position. Just as Maigret and Mr. Pyke were sitting down on the terrace they saw Monsieur Émile, more of a little white mouse than ever, advancing onto the square with short steps, a panama hat on his head, and heading diagonally for the post office—situated to the left of the church, at the top. The door was open. Four or five people were waiting, while the postmistress sorted the mail.

It was Saturday, Jojo was giving the red tiles of the dining room a good wash; her feet were bare, and rivulets of dirty water were draining onto the terrace.

Paul brought not two glasses of white wine, but a whole bottle.

"Do you know the woman who went up to Charlot's room?"

"That's his girlfriend."

"Is she in service?"

"I don't think so. She's some sort of a dancer or singer in a Marseilles nightclub. It's the third or fourth time she's been here."

"He telephoned her?"

"Yesterday afternoon, while you were in your room."

"Do you know what he said?"

"He simply asked her to come and spend the week-end. She accepted at once."

"Were Charlot and Marcellin friends?"

"I don't remember having seen them together; I mean just the two of them."

"I would like you to try to remember exactly. When, that evening, Marcellin mentioned me . . . ."

"I know what you mean. Your inspector put the same question to me."

"I suppose at the start of the evening the customers were at different tables, like yesterday evening?"

"Yes. It always starts off like that."

"Do you know what happened next?"

"Someone put on the gramophone, I don't recall who. The Dutchman and his girlfriend began to dance. It comes back to me because I noticed that she let herself go limp in his arms like a rag doll."

"Did other people dance too?"

"Mrs. Wilcox and Monsieur Philippe. He's a very good dancer."

"Where was Marcellin at that moment?"

"I seem to picture him at the bar."

"Very drunk?"

"Not very, but fairly. Wait. A detail. He insisted on asking Mrs. Wilcox to dance . . ."

"Marcellin?"

Was it deliberate that when his compatriot was mentioned Mr. Pyke suddenly looked blank?

"Did she accept?"

"They danced a few steps. Marcellin must have stumbled. He liked to act the clown when there were a lot of people present. It was she who stood the first round of drinks. Yes. There was a bottle of whisky on their table. She doesn't like being served by the glass. Marcellin drank some and asked for white wine."

"And the major?"

"I was just thinking of him. He was in the opposite corner and I'm trying to remember who he had with him. I think it was Polyte."

"Who's Polyte?"

"A Morin. The one with the green boat. In the summer he takes tourists right round the island. He wears a proper captain's cap."

"Is he a captain?"

"He did his service in the navy and he must hold the rank of quartermaster. He often accompanies the major to Toulon. The dentist was drinking with them. Marcellin started going from one table to the other, with his glass, and, if I am not mistaken, he was mixing whisky with his white wine."

"How was it he began talking about me? Who to? Was it at the major's table, or Mrs. Wilcox's?"

"I'm doing my best. You saw for yourself how it is, and yesterday was a quiet evening. The Dutch couple were near Mrs. Wilcox. I think it was at that table that the conversation began. Marcellin was standing up, in the middle of the room, when I heard him declare:

"'*My friend Chief Inspector Maigret . . . Just so, my friend, and I know what I'm talking about . . . I can prove it . . .*'"

"He produced a letter?"

"Not to my knowledge. I was busy, with Jojo, serving."

"Was your wife in the room?"

"I think she'd gone up. She normally does go up when she has finished the accounts. She's not very strong and needs plenty of sleep."

"In short Marcellin might just as well have been addressing Major Bellam as Mrs. Wilcox or the Dutchman? And even Charlot, or someone else? The dentist, for example? Monsieur Émile?"

"I suppose so."

He was called inside and, excusing himself, left them. The people coming out of the post office began to saunter across the sunny patch of the square where, in one corner, a woman was standing behind a table on which vegetables were for sale. The mayor, to one side of the Arche, was unpacking his crates.

"You're wanted on the telephone, Monsieur Maigret."

He penetrated the semidarkness of the café, picked up the receiver.

"That you, chief? Lechat here. It's all over. I'm in a bar near the cemetery. The woman, you know who, is with me. She hasn't left me since the *Cormorant*. She has had time to tell me her life story."

"How did it go off?"

"Very well. She bought some flowers. Other people

from the island placed some on his grave. It was very hot in the cemetery. I don't know what to do. I think I shall have to ask her to lunch."

"Can she hear you?"

"No. I'm in a telephone booth. I can see her through the window. She's powdering her nose and looking into a pocket mirror."

"She hasn't met anyone? Or telephoned?"

"She hasn't left me for a second. I even had to go with her to the florist and, behind the hearse, as I was walking beside her, I looked as though I was part of the family."

"Did you take the bus to get from Giens to Hyères?"

"The only thing I could do was to ask her to come with me in my car. Everything going all right, on the island?"

"Everything's all right."

When he came back onto the terrace, Maigret found the dentist sitting beside Mr. Pyke and apparently waiting to share the bottle of white wine.

Philippe de Moricourt, a pile of newspapers under his arm, was hesitating whether to come into the Arche.

Monsieur Émile, with cautious steps, was heading toward his villa where old Justine would be waiting for him, and, as on any other day, the smell of bouillabaisse floated out from the kitchen.

7

It wasn't a nickname. The fat girl hadn't done it on purpose. She really had been called Aglaé at her christening. She was very fat, especially the bottom half, deformed like a woman of fifty or sixty who has become fat with age and, by contrast, her face only looked the more infantile, for Aglaé was twenty-six years old at most.

Maigret had discovered, that afternoon, a whole new section of Porquerolles when, still accompanied by Mr. Pyke, he had walked right across the square for the first time to pay a visit to the post office. Was there really a smell of incense coming from the church, where the services could not have been very frequent?

It was the same square as the one opposite the Arche, and yet one would have sworn that, at the top, the air was hotter and more dense. Some small gardens, in front of two or three houses, were a riot of flowers and bees. The noises from the harbor reached them muted. Two old men were playing boules, *pétanque-*

style, that is without sending the jack more than a few
yards from their feet, and it was strange to see the pre-
cautions they took in bending down.

One of them was Ferdinand Galli, the patriarch of
all the Gallis on the island, who kept a café in this corner of the square, a café which the chief inspector had
never seen anyone enter. It must only have been fre-
quented by neighbors, or by the Gallis of the tribe. His
partner was a retired man, natty, completely deaf, wearing a railwayman's cap, and another octogenarian, sitting on the post-office bench, was watching them sleepily.

For beside the open door of the post office there was
a green painted bench on which Maigret was to spend a
part of his afternoon.

"I wondered if you would come up here in the end!"
Aglaé exclaimed, seeing him come in. "I expected you
would need to use the telephone and wouldn't want to
do it from the Arche, where so many people can hear
what you are saying."

"Will it take long to get Paris, mademoiselle?"

"With a priority call I can get you through in a few
minutes."

"In that case, get Police Headquarters for me."

"I know the number. It was me that put your inspector through when he called you."

He all but asked:

"And you listened in?"

But she would not be long in revealing this herself.

"Who do you wish to speak to at Police Head-quarters?"

"Sergeant Lucas. If he's not there, Inspector Torrence."

A few seconds later he had Lucas on the line.

"What's the weather like with you, old man? Still raining? Showers? Good! Listen, Lucas. Do your best to get me everything you can as soon as possible on some-one called Philippe de Moricourt. Yes. Lechat has seen his papers and says it's his real name. His last address in Paris was a furnished house on the Left Bank, Rue Jacob, 17b . . . What do I want to know exactly? I've got no preconceived ideas. Everything you can find out. I don't think he's got a dossier in the Records, but you can always check. Do all you can by telephone and then call me back here. No number. Just Porquerolles. I would also like you to telephone the police at Ostend. Ask if they know a certain Bebelmans who, I think, is an important shipbuilder. Same thing. Everything you can find out. That's not all. Don't cut us off, mademoi-selle. Have you any acquaintances in Montparnasse? See what they say about a certain Jef de Greef, who is a sort of painter and spent a certain amount of time on the Seine, in his boat moored near the Pont Marie. Have you made a note of that? That's all, yes. Don't wait for all the information before ringing me back. Put as many people on to it as you like. Everything all right, at the office? . . . *Who*'s had a baby? . . . Janvier's wife? . . . Give him my congratulations."

When he came out of the telephone box, he saw Aglaé, without a trace of embarrassment, taking the earphones off her head.

"You always listen in to conversations?"

"I stayed on the line in case it was cut off. I don't trust the Hyères operator; she's an old cat."

"Do you do the same for everyone?"

"In the morning I haven't time because of the mail, but in the afternoon it's easier."

"Do you take note of the calls made by the islanders?"

"I have to."

"Could you make me out a list of all the calls you have put through in the last few days? Say the last eight days."

"Right away. It'll take me a few minutes."

"You're the person who receives the telegrams as well, aren't you?"

"There aren't many, except in the season. I had one this morning which is sure to interest you."

"How do you know?"

"It's a telegram which someone sent from here, someone who appears to be interested in one of the people, at least, about whom you've been asking for information."

"Have you a copy?"

"I'll find it for you."

A moment later she was handing a form to the inspector, who read:

Fred Masson, c/o Angelo, Rue Blanche, Paris.

Like complete information on Philippe de Moricourt address Rue Jacob Paris stop *Please telegraph Porquerolles. Regards.*
Signed: CHARLOT.

Maigret gave it to Mr. Pyke to read, and the latter confined himself to a nod.

"Will you prepare a list of the calls for me, mademoiselle? I'll wait outside with my friend."

So it was that, for the first time, they went and sat on the bench, in the shade of the eucalyptus trees round the square, and the wall at their backs was pink and hot. Somewhere there was an invisible fig tree, and they inhaled its sweet smell.

"In a few minutes," said Mr. Pyke, looking at the church clock, "I shall ask your permission to leave you for a moment, if you don't mind."

Was it from politeness that he pretended to believe that Maigret would grieve over it?

"The major has invited me for a drink at about five o'clock. I should have hurt his feelings by refusing."

"That's perfectly all right."

"I thought you would probably be busy."

Hardly time for the chief inspector to smoke a pipe, as he watched the two old men playing boules, before Aglaé was calling out in her shrill voice, over the counter:

"Monsieur Maigret! It's ready!"

He went and took the piece of paper which she was

holding out to him, and went and sat once more beside
the man from the Yard.

She had done her work conscientiously, in the la-
bored writing of a schoolgirl, with three or four spelling
mistakes.

The word "butcher" recurred several times on the
list. Apparently he telephoned every day to Hyères to
order his meat for the next day. Then there was the Cooperative, with calls as frequent but more varied.

Maigret made a mark a little more than halfway
down the list, thus separating the calls made before
Marcellin's death from those made afterwards.

"Are you taking notes?" Mr. Pyke asked, seeing his
companion opening a large notebook.

Didn't this imply that for the first time he was seeing
Maigret behaving like a real chief inspector?

The name which occurred most often on the list was
Justine's. She called Nice, Marseilles, Béziers, Avignon,
and in one week there were four calls to Paris.

"We'll see about that presently," said Maigret. "I
suppose the postmistress took care to listen in. Is that
done in England too?"

"I don't think it's legal, but it's possible that it sometimes happens."

The day before, Charlot had telephoned Marseilles.
Maigret knew that already. It was to summon his
girlfriend, whom they had seen landing from the *Cormorant* and with whom he was now playing cards on
the terrace of the Arche.

For the Arche could be seen in the distance, with human forms bustling around it. From where they were, where all was so calm, it looked as active as a hive of bees.

The most interesting thing was that Marcellin's name occurred on the list. He had called a number in Nice, just two days before his death.

Suddenly Maigret rose and went into the post office, and Mr. Pyke followed him in.

"Do you know what this number is, mademoiselle?"

"Certainly. It's the house where the lady works. Justine calls it every day; you can see it on the list."

"Have you listened in to Justine's conversations?"

"Often. I no longer bother, because it's always the same."

"Does she do the talking, or her son?"

"She talks and Monsieur Émile listens."

"I don't understand."

"She's deaf. So Monsieur Émile holds the receiver to his ear, and repeats what is being said to her. Then she shouts so loud into the mouthpiece that it's difficult to distinguish her syllables. The first thing she says is always:

"'How much?'

"They give her the figure for the takings. Monsieur Émile, standing by her, notes it down. She calls up her houses one after the other."

"I suppose it's Ginette who answers in Nice?"

"Yes, seeing that she's the manageress."

"And the Paris calls?"

"There are fewer of them. Always to the same person, a certain Monsieur Louis. And always to ask for girls. He gives the age and the price. She answers yes or no. Sometimes she does her business as though she were at the village market."

"You haven't ever noticed anything odd about her conversations recently? Monsieur Émile hasn't telephoned privately?"

"I don't think he'd dare."

"Doesn't his mother allow him?"

"She hardly allows him to do anything."

"And Marcellin?"

"I was just going to tell you about him. It was unusual for him to come to the post office, and then it was only to cash money orders. I should say that in a year he would only telephone three times."

"To whom?"

"Once, it was to Toulon to order a part of a motor, which he needed for his boat. Another time it was to Nice . . ."

"To Ginette?"

"It was to say that he hadn't been able to cash the order. He received one almost every month, did you know? She had made a mistake. The sum in words wasn't the same as the sum in figures, and I couldn't pay him. She sent another by the next post."

"How long ago was this?"

"About three months. The door was closed, which means it was cold, so it was winter."

"And the last call?"

"I started to listen, as usual, then Madame Galli came in to buy some stamps."

"Was it a long conversation?"

"Longer than usual. It's easy to check up."

She turned over the pages of her book.

"Two three-minute periods."

"You heard the start. What did Marcellin say?"

"Something like this:

"Is that you? . . . It's me . . . yes. No, it's not money . . . Money, I could have as much of that as I wanted . . .'"

"Did she say anything?"

"She murmured:

"You've been drinking again, Marcellin.'

"He swore he was practically sober. He went on:

"I want you to do something for me . . . Is there a big Larousse in the house?'

"That's all I know. At that moment Madame Galli came in and she's not easy to please. She says it's she who pays for civil servants with her taxes and she's always talking of complaining."

"As the call only lasted six minutes, it's unlikely that Ginette had time to look up the *Larousse* encyclopedia, come back to the telephone, and give Marcellin a reply."

"She sent the reply by telegram. Look! I have it here for you."

She gave him a yellow form on which he read:

Died in 1890.

It was signed: *Ginette.*

"It would have been too bad for you if you hadn't come up to see me, wouldn't it? I shouldn't have come down, and you would have found out nothing."

"Did you notice Marcellin's face when he read this telegram?"

"He reread it two or three times, to make sure he had got it right, then he went off whistling."

"As though he had received some good news?"

"Exactly. And also, I think, as if he had suddenly been struck with admiration for somebody."

"Did you listen to Charlot's conversation yesterday?"

"With Bébé?"

"I beg your pardon?"

"He calls her Bébé. She must have arrived this morning. You want me to repeat his words?

"He said to her: 'How goes, Bébé? I'm fine, thanks. I've got to stick around here a few more days and I'd like a little bit of fun. So come on over.'"

"And she came," Maigret finished. "Thank you very much, mademoiselle. I'm on the bench outside, with my friend, and I'm waiting for my call from Paris."

Three-quarters of an hour was passed watching the boules; the young married couple came to send off postcards; the butcher in turn came to make his daily call to

Hyères. Mr. Pyke looked at the church tower from time to time. Occasionally he opened his mouth as well, perhaps to ask a question, but each time he changed his mind.

They were both of them oppressed by the heavily scented heat. From afar they could see the men gathering for the big boules match, the one between about ten players, fought out across the entire square until time for apéritifs and dinner.

The dentist was taking part. The *Cormorant* had left the island for Giens Point from whence it would bring back Inspector Lechat and Ginette.

Finally Aglaé's voice summoned him in.

"Paris!" she announced.

It was the good Lucas who must, as usual during Maigret's absences, have taken over the latter's office. Through the window Lucas could see the Seine and the Pont Saint-Michel, while the chief inspector was looking vaguely at Aglaé.

"I've got part of the information, chief. I'm expecting the rest from Ostend presently. Who shall I start with?"

"Whichever you like."

"Right, the Moricourt fellow. That wasn't difficult. Torrence remembered the name through having seen it on the cover of a book. It's his real name all right. His father, who was a cavalry captain, died a long while ago. His mother lives at Saumur. As far as I could gather they haven't any private means. Several times

Philippe de Moricourt tried to marry heiresses, but didn't succeed."

Aglaé was listening unashamedly, and through the glass, was winking at Maigret, to underline the bits she liked.

"He passes himself off as a man of letters. He published two volumes of poetry with a publisher on the Left Bank. He used to frequent the Café de Flore, where he was fairly well known. He has also worked occasionally on several newspapers. Is that what you want to know?"

"Go on."

"I've hardly any other details as I did it all by telephone, to save time; but I sent someone to find out and you'll have some more snippets this evening or tomorrow. There's never been any charge against him, or rather there was one, five years ago, but it was withdrawn."

"I'm listening."

"A woman, who lives in Auteuil, whose name I should be able to get, had given him a rare edition to sell, after which she waited for several months without hearing of him. She lodged a complaint. It was found that he had sold the book to an American. As for the money, he promised to pay it back in monthly instalments. I got its former owner on the telephone. Moricourt was habitually two or three payments behind, but he paid up in the end, bit by bit."

"Is that all?"

"Almost. You know the type. Always well dressed, always impeccably correct."

"And with old women?"

"Nothing definite. He had dealings of which he made a great mystery."

"And the other one?"

"Did you know they knew one another? It seems de Greef is quite somebody; some people claim that, if he wanted, he could be one of the best painters of his generation."

"And he doesn't want to be?"

"He ends by quarrelling with everybody. He went off with a Belgian girl of very good family."

"I know."

"Good. When he arrived in Paris, he held an exhibition of his works in a small room in the Rue de Seine. On the last day, as he hadn't sold anything, he burned all the canvases. Some say veritable orgies took place on board his boat. He has illustrated several erotic works which are sold under the counter. It's mainly off this that he lived. There you are, chief. I'm waiting for Ostend to call. Everything all right, down there?"

Through the glass, Mr. Pyke was showing Maigret his watch, and as it was five o'clock, he went off in the direction of the major's villa.

The chief inspector felt quite light-headed about it, regarding it like a spell of holidays.

"Did you convey my congratulations to Janvier?

Ring up my wife and tell her to go and see his and take something along, a present or some flowers. But not a silver mug!"

He found himself back with Aglaé, separated from her by the grilled partition. She seemed very amused. She admitted without shame:

"I'd like to see one of his books. Do you think he has some on board?"

Then, without stopping:

"It's strange! Your job's a lot simpler than people think. Information pours in from all sides. Do you think it's one of those two?"

There was a large bunch of mimosa on her desk, and a bag of sweets, which she offered to the chief inspector.

"Things happen so seldom here! About Monsieur Philippe, I forgot to tell you that he writes a lot. I don't read his letters, naturally. He shoves them in the box and I recognize his writing and his ink, as he always uses green ink. I don't know why."

"Who does he write to?"

"I forget the names, but it's nearly always to Paris. Now and then he writes to his mother. The letters to Paris are much thicker."

"Does he get much post in return?"

"Quite a lot. And reviews, and newspapers. Every day there's printed matter for him."

"Mrs. Wilcox?"

"She writes a lot as well, to England, Capri, Egypt. I

particularly remember Egypt because I took the liberty of asking her for the stamps for my nephew."

"Does she telephone?"

"She has been along to telephone two or three times from the box, and each time it was London she was calling. Unfortunately I don't understand English."

She added:

"I'm going to shut up. I should have shut at five. But if you want to wait for your call . . ."

"What call?"

"Didn't Monsieur Lucas say he would call back about Ostend?"

She probably wasn't dangerous; yet Maigret would have preferred, if only because of the people nearby, not to remain too long alone with her. She was all curiosity. She asked him, for example:

"Aren't you going to telephone your wife?"

He told her he would be on the square, not far from the Arche in case a call came for him, and he went down quietly, smoking his pipe, in the direction of the boules match. He no longer needed to watch his behavior, as Mr. Pyke was not there to observe him. He really wanted to play boules and several times he asked about the rules of the game.

He was extremely surprised to discover that the dentist, whom everyone familiarly addressed as Léon, was a first-class player. At twenty yards, after three bounding strides he would strike his opponent's ball and send it rolling away into the distance, and each time he at once affected a little modest air as though he considered the achievement to be quite natural.

The chief inspector went to have a glass of wine and found Charlot busy working the fruit machine while his companion on the bench was engrossed in a film magazine. Had they had their "little bit of fun"?

"Isn't your friend with you?" asked Paul in surprise.

For Mr. Pyke as well, it must have been like a holiday. He was with another Englishman. He could speak his own language, use expressions which only meant something to two men from the same school.

It was easy to foretell the arrival of the *Cormorant*. Each time the same phenomenon took place. Outside there was a sort of downward current. People could be seen passing by, all making for the harbor. Then, once the boat was moored, the ebb would begin. The same people would pass by in the opposite direction, with, in addition, the new arrivals carrying suitcases or packages.

He followed the downward current, not far from the mayor who was pushing his eternal wheelbarrow. On the boat deck he at once saw Ginette and the inspector, who looked like a couple of friends. There were also fishermen coming back from the funeral and two old ladies, tourists for the Grand Hôtel.

In the group of people watching the disembarkation, he recognized Charlot, who had followed him and who, like him, seemed to be going through a ritual without really believing in it.

"Nothing new, chief?" asked Lechat, no sooner had he set foot on land. "If you knew how hot it was over there!"

"Did it go off all right?"

Ginette stayed with them, quite naturally. She appeared tired. Her look betrayed a certain anxiety.

The three of them set off toward the Arche, and Maigret had the feeling that he had been taking this walk daily for a very long time.

"Are you thirsty, Ginette?"

"I could do with an apéritif."

They drank together, on the terrace, and Ginette was uncomfortable every time she felt Maigret's gaze fall upon her. He looked at her dreamily, heavily, like a person whose thoughts are far away.

"I'll go up and wash," she announced when her glass was empty.

"May I come with you?"

Lechat, who sensed something new in the air, was trying to guess. He didn't dare question his chief. He remained alone at the table, while the latter, behind Ginette, climbed the stairs.

"You know," she said, when they were finally in the bedroom, "I really want to change my life."

"That doesn't worry me."

She pretended to joke.

"And supposing it worried me?"

Nonetheless she removed her hat, then her dress, which he helped her to unfasten at the back.

"This has sort of done something to me," she sighed. "I think he was happy here."

On the other evenings Marcellin, at this hour, would have been taking part in the game of boules on the square, in the setting sun.

"Everyone's been very kind. He was well liked."

She hastily removed her corsets, which had left deep marks on her milky skin. Maigret, facing the attic window, had his back to her.

"Do you remember the question I asked you?" he said in a neutral voice.

"You repeated it enough times. I would never have believed you could be so hard."

"On my side I would never have believed that you would try to hide anything from me."

"Have I hidden something from you?"

"I asked you why you had come here, to Porquerolles, when Marcel's body was already in Hyères."

"I answered you."

"You told me a lie."

"I don't know what you mean."

"Why didn't you tell me about the telephone call?"

"What telephone call?"

"The one Marcellin made to you the day before he died."

"I didn't remember it."

"Nor the telegram?"

He didn't have to turn round to discover her reaction, and kept his gaze fixed on the game of boules in progress opposite the terrace, from where there came a murmur of voices. The clink of glasses could be heard.

It was very soft, very reassuring, and Mr. Pyke wasn't there. As the silence continued, behind him, he asked:

"What are you thinking about?"

"I'm thinking that I was wrong, as you know perfectly well."

"Are you dressed?"

"Just going to put on my dress."

He went and opened the door, to make sure there was nobody in the corridor. When he came back to the middle of the room, Ginette was busy rearranging her hair in front of the mirror.

"You didn't mention the *Larousse*?"

"Who to?"

"I don't know. Monsieur Émile for example. Or Charlot."

"I wasn't so stupid as to mention it."

"Because you were hoping to step into Marcel's shoes? Do you know, Ginette, you are a terribly calculating woman."

"That's what people always say about women when they try to provide for the future. And they fall on them when misery drives them into a job they haven't chosen."

There was a sudden bitterness in her voice.

"I thought you were going to marry Monsieur Émile?"

"On condition Justine makes up her mind to die and doesn't make last-minute arrangements preventing her son from marrying. Perhaps you think that makes me feel happy!"

"In short, if Marcel's tip was a good one and you succeeded, you wouldn't marry?"

"Certainly not that piece of creeping sickness."

"Would you leave the house at Nice?"

"Without a moment's hesitation, I assure you."

"What would you do?"

"I'd go and live in the country, anywhere. I'd keep chickens and rabbits."

"What did Marcellin say to you on the telephone?"

"You'll say I'm lying again."

He stared at her for a long while, and then said quietly: "Not anymore."

"Good! It's not a moment too soon. He said he had accidentally discovered an extraordinary thing. Those are the words he used. He added that it could mean big money, but he wasn't yet sure."

"Did he make any reference to anyone?"

"No. I have never known him to be so mysterious. He needed some information. He asked if we had a big *Larousse*, the one in I don't know how many volumes, in the house. I said we didn't keep one. Then he insisted on my going to the town library to look it up."

"What did he want to know?"

"It's just too bad, isn't it? Now you've got so far, I haven't a chance of course."

"None at all."

"Even though I didn't understand a thing about it. I thought I'd get some idea when I reached here."

"Who died in 1890?"

"You've seen my telegram? Didn't he destroy it?"

"The post office, as usual, kept a copy."

"A certain van Gogh, a painter. I read that he committed suicide. He was very poor and today people fight over his pictures, which are worth I don't know what. I wondered if Marcel had got hold of one."

"And it wasn't that?"

"I don't think so. When he telephoned me he didn't even know the gentleman concerned was dead."

"What did you think?"

"I don't know, I promise. Only I told myself that if Marcel could make money with this information, it was possible that I could do so too. Especially when I learned that he had been killed. People don't kill for fun. He had no enemies. There was nothing to steal from him. You understand?"

"You assume the crime has a connection with the van Gogh in question?"

Maigret spoke without a trace of irony. He took small puffs at his pipe and gazed out of the window.

"No doubt you were right."

"Too late, since you're here and it's no more use to me. Is there any further reason to keep me on the island? You see it's a holiday for me here, and as long as you keep me here, the old cat can't say anything."

"In that case, stay."

"Thank you. You are becoming almost like you were when I knew you in Paris."

He didn't trouble to return the compliment.

"You have a rest."

He went downstairs, passed near to Charlot who surveyed him with a bantering eye, and went and sat beside Lechat, on the terrace.

It was the most luscious hour of the day. The whole island was relaxed, and the sea around it, the rocks, the ground of the square, which seemed to breathe to another rhythm after the heat of the daytime.

"Have you found out anything, chief?"

Maigret's first thought was to order a drink from Jojo, who was passing nearby and who looked as if she were cross with him for having closeted himself with Ginette in the bedroom.

"I'm afraid so," he sighed finally.

And, as the inspector was looking at him in surprise:

"I mean that I shall probably not have much longer to stay here. It's a good place, don't you think? On the other hand, there's Mr. Pyke."

Wasn't a quick success better, on account of Mr. Pyke, and what he would say at Scotland Yard?

"There's a call from Paris for you, Monsieur Maigret."

It was probably the information from Ostend.

8

Sunday lay so heavily in the air as to become almost nauseating. Maigret used to claim openly, half seriously, half in fun, that he had always had the knack of sensing a Sunday from his bed, without even having to open his eyes.

Here there was an unprecedented noise of bells. They were not proper church bells, but small, high-pitched ones, like chapel or convent bells. One was led to the belief that the quality, the density of the air was not the same as elsewhere. One could distinctly hear the hammer striking the bronze, which gave out some sort of a note, but it was then that the phenomenon would begin: a first ring would carry into the pale and still cool sky, would extend hesitantly, like a smoke ring, becoming a perfect circle out of which other circles would form by magic, ever increasing, ever purer. The circles passed beyond the square and the houses, stretched over the harbor and a long way out to sea where small boats were anchored. One felt them above the hills and rocks, and they hadn't ceased to be perceptible before the hammer struck the metal once more and other circles of sound were born so as to reproduce themselves, then others, which one listened to in innocent amazement, as one watches a firework.

Even the simple sound of footsteps on the rough surface of the square had something paschal about it, and Maigret, glancing out of the window, was expecting to see first communicants with their small legs becoming caught up in their veils.

As on the previous day he put on his slippers and trousers, and slipped his jacket over his nightshirt with the red embroidered collar, went downstairs and, going into the kitchen, was thoroughly disappointed. Subconsciously he had been hoping to repeat the previous early morning, to find himself beside the stove again with Jojo preparing the coffee, and the clear rectangle of the door open to the outside. But today there were four or five fishermen there. They must have been given some liquor, which was strongly pervading the air. On the floor of the room a basket of fish had been upset: pink hogfish, blue and green fish of which Maigret didn't know the name, a sort of sea serpent with red and yellow blotches, which was still alive and coiling itself round the foot of a chair.

"Do you want a cup of coffee, Monsieur Maigret?"

It wasn't Jojo who served him but the *patron*. Perhaps because it was Sunday. Maigret felt like a thwarted child.

———

It sometimes happened to him, especially in the morning, especially when he approached the mirror to shave. He would look at the broad face, the huge eyes often underlined with pouches, the thinning hair. He would become stern, deliberately, as though to frighten himself. He would tell himself:

"That's the divisional chief inspector!"

Who would have dared not to take him seriously? Heaps of people, who did not have easy consciences, trembled at the mention of his name. He had the power to question them until they cried out with anguish, to put them in prison, send them to the guillotine.

In this very island, there was now someone who, like himself, heard the sound of the bells, who breathed the Sabbath air, someone who was drinking in the same room as himself the previous evening and who, in a few days, would be shut up once and for all within four walls.

He swallowed down his cup of coffee, poured himself out another, which he carried up to his room, and he had some difficulty in realizing that all this could be serious: it was not so very long ago that he was wearing short trousers and walking across his village square, on chilly mornings, his fingertips numb with cold, to go and serve Mass in the small church lit only by wax candles.

Now he was a grown-up: everyone believed what he said, and there was only himself whom, from time to time, it was hard to convince.

Did other people have the same experience? Did Mr.

Pyke, for example, sometimes wonder how other people could take him seriously? Did he, be it ever so rarely, have the impression that it was all a game, that life was just a joke?

Was the major anything more than an overgrown schoolboy, like the ones there are in every class, one of those fat and sleepy boys whom the master cannot resist making fun of?

Mr. Pyke had said a terrible thing the previous evening, shortly before the Polyte episode. It was downstairs, at the moment when, as on the evening before and every other evening, almost everybody was gathered at the Arche. Naturally, the Yard inspector had sat at the major's table, and at that moment, despite the difference in age and rotundity, they had a sort of family resemblance.

They must have been drinking, late in the afternoon, when Mr. Pyke had been to see his fellow countryman at the villa. Enough to have a dulled eye and thick tongue, but too little to lose their dignity. Not only had they been taught the same manners at school, but later, heaven knows where, they had learned to hold liquor in the same way.

They were not sad, but nostalgic rather, a little faraway. They gave the impression of being two gods gazing down on the agitation of the world with a condescending melancholy, and, just as Maigret sat down next to him, Mr. Pyke had sighed:

"She's been a grandmother since last week."

He did not look at the person in question, whose name he always avoided mentioning, but it could only be Mrs. Wilcox. She was there, on the far side of the room, sitting on the bench in Philippe's company. The Dutchman and Anna were at the next table.

Mr. Pyke had allowed a certain time to elapse, then had added in the same neutral voice:

"Her daughter and son-in-law don't allow her to set foot in England. The major knows them extremely well."

Poor old woman! For all of a sudden, Mrs. Wilcox was revealed as really an old woman. One stopped laughing at her makeup, her dyed hair—with the white roots visible—and her artificial animation.

She was a grandmother, and Maigret remembered that he had conjured up his own in his thoughts; he had tried to imagine his reactions as a child if he had been shown a woman like Mrs. Wilcox and told:

"Go and kiss your granny!"

She was forbidden to live in her own country and she made no protest. She knew perfectly well that she wouldn't have the last word, that it was she who was in the wrong. Like drunkards, who are given a bare minimum of pocket money, and who try to cheat, and cadge a drink here and there.

Did she, like drunks too, sometimes become emotional over her misfortunes, weep in a corner by herself?

Perhaps when she had had a lot to drink? For she used to drink as well. Her Philippe saw to the filling of her glass whenever the need arose, while Anna, on the same bench, was only thinking of one thing: the moment when she could finally go off to bed.

Maigret was shaving. He hadn't been able to get into the only bathroom, which Ginette was occupying.

"In five minutes!" she had called out to him through the door.

From time to time he glanced out on to the square, which was not the same color as on other days, even now that the bells had ceased. The priest was in the middle of saying the first Mass. The one in his village used to rattle it off so quickly that young Maigret had scarcely time to get in the responses as he ran about with the cruets.

An odd sort of job, his! He was only a man like the others, and he held the fate of other men in his hands.

He had looked at them one by one, the evening before. He hadn't drunk much, just enough to exaggerate his feelings ever so slightly. De Greef, with his clear-cut profile, stared at him from time to time in silent irony and seemed to be challenging him. Philippe, despite his fine name and his ancestors, was of a coarser stock, and he tried hard to cut a figure each time Mrs. Wilcox ordered him about like a servant.

He must have got his revenge at other moments, granted, but he was nonetheless obliged to swallow insults in public.

The one he swallowed was fair-sized, so much so in fact that everyone felt uncomfortable about it. Poor Paul, who fortunately didn't know where the source of the trouble had been, took infinite pains afterwards to bring the party back to life.

They must be talking about it, down there. They would talk about it on the island all day. Would Polyte keep the secret? Just then it hardly mattered.

Polyte was at the counter, his captain's cap on his head, and he had already consumed a good many short drinks; he spoke so loud that his voice was drowning the various conversations. On Mrs. Wilcox's orders, Philippe had crossed the room to start up the gramophone, as often happened.

Then, with a wink at Maigret, Polyte had headed in turn toward the machine and stopped it.

Then he had turned to Moricourt and looked at him sarcastically, straight in the eye.

Philippe, without protesting, had pretended not to notice.

"I don't like people looking at me like that!" Polyte had then shouted out, advancing a few paces.

"But . . . I'm not even looking at you . . ."

"So you're too grand to look at me?"

"I didn't say that."

"You think I don't understand?"

Mrs. Wilcox had murmured something in English to her companion. Mr. Pyke had frowned.

"I'm not good enough for you, perhaps, you little rat?"

Very red in the face, Philippe still didn't move, making an effort to look elsewhere.

"Try saying again that I'm not good enough for you."

At the same moment de Greef had looked at Maigret, sharply, in a particularly pointed way. Had he understood? Lechat, who had understood nothing at all, had wanted to get up and interrupt, and Maigret had been obliged to seize his wrist under the table.

"What would you say if I pushed your pretty face in, eh? What would you say?"

Polyte, who judged that the ground was sufficiently prepared, then brought his fist flying over the table, at Philippe's face.

The latter put his hand up to his nose. But that was all. He didn't try to defend himself, nor to attack in his turn. He stammered:

"I've done nothing to you."

Mrs. Wilcox was calling out, facing the bar:

"Monsieur Paul! Monsieur Paul! Will you throw this hooligan out? It's an outrage."

Her accent gave a special flavor to the words "hooligan" and "outrage."

"As for you . . ." Polyte began, turning to the Dutchman.

The reaction was different. Without leaving his place, de Greef stiffened, growled:

"That's enough, Polyte!"

One could feel that he wouldn't let himself be trifled with, that he was ready to spring, with all his muscles tensed.

Paul finally interposed.

"Calm down, Polyte. Come into the kitchen for a moment. I want a word with you."

The captain let himself be led off, protesting for the sake of appearances.

Lechat, who still hadn't understood, had however asked, dreamily:

"Was it you, chief?"

Maigret had not replied. He had assumed as benign an air as possible when the Scotland Yard inspector had looked him in the eye.

Paul had made his apologies in the correct way. Polyte was put out of the back door and seen no more. Today he would act like a hero.

The fact remained that Philippe hadn't defended himself, that his face, for one moment, had sweated with fear, a physical fear which seizes the pit of the stomach and is not to be overcome.

After that he had drunk to excess, with a cloudy look on his face, and Mrs. Wilcox had finally taken him off.

Nothing else had happened. Charlot and his dancing girl had gone up to bed rather early, and when Maigret had in turn gone up, they were still not asleep. Ginette and Monsieur Émile had chatted in undertones. No one had offered drinks all round, perhaps on account of the incident.

"Come in, Lechat," the chief inspector called out through the door.

The inspector was already fully dressed.

"Has Mr. Pyke gone for a swim?"

"He's downstairs, busy eating his bacon and eggs. I went down to see the *Cormorant* off."

"Nothing to report?"

"Nothing. It seems that on Sundays lots of people come over from Hyères and Toulon, people who rush for the beaches and strew them with sardine tins and empty bottles. We'll be able to see them landing in an hour."

The information from Ostend contained nothing unexpected. Monsieur Bebelmans, Anna's father, was an important figure, who had been mayor of the town for a long time and had once stood for Parliament. Since his daughter's departure, he had forbidden her name to be mentioned in his presence. His wife was dead, and Anna hadn't been told of it.

"It seems that everyone who has come off the rails for one reason or another has landed up here," Maigret observed as he put on his coat.

"It's the climate that's responsible!" riposted the inspector, who was not troubled by such questions. "I went to see another revolver this morning."

He carried out his job conscientiously. He had taken pains to find out all the revolver owners. He went to see them one after the other, examined their weapons, without too much hope, simply because that was part of the routine.

"What are we doing today?"

Maigret, making for the door, avoided replying, and they found Mr. Pyke in front of the red check tablecloth.

"I presume you are a Protestant?" he said to him. "In which case you wouldn't go to High Mass?"

"I am a Protestant and I went to Low Mass."

Perhaps he would have done just the same if there had only been a synagogue, so as to attend a service, whatever it was, because it was Sunday.

"I don't know whether you'll want to come with me. This morning I have to pay a call on a lady you aren't anxious to meet."

"You're going aboard the yacht?"

Maigret nodded, and Mr. Pyke pushed his plate away, rose, and picked up the straw hat he had bought the day before at the mayor's shop, for he was already sunburnt enough to make his face almost as red as the major's.

"Are you coming with me?"

"You may need a translator."

"Shall I come too?" asked Lechat.

"I'd like you to, yes. Can you row?"

"I was born at the seaside."

They walked as far as the harbor, once again. It was the inspector who asked a fisherman permission to use a boat without a motor, and the three men took their places in it. They could see de Greef and Anna breakfasting on the deck of their little boat.

The sea, too, as though in honor of the Sabbath, had put on a shot-satin appearance, and at every stroke of the oar pearls sparkled in the sun. The *Cormorant* was on the other side of the water, at Giens Point, waiting for the passengers to alight from the bus. One could see the bottom of the sea, the violet urchins in the hollow of the rocks and an occasional brightly colored sea wolf which would flee like an arrow. The bells were ringing to announce High Mass, and all the houses must have smelled of the scent the women put on their best dresses, in addition to the morning coffee.

The *North Star* seemed much bigger, much higher from alongside, and as nobody was stirring, Lechat called out, raising his head:

"Hello there, on board!"

After a fairly long pause, a sailor leaned over the rail, one cheek covered with frothy soap, an open razor in his hand.

"Can we see your mistress?"

"Couldn't you come back in an hour or so?"

Mr. Pyke was visibly uncomfortable. Maigret hesitated a moment, thinking of the "grandmother."

"We'll wait on deck if necessary," he said to the seaman. "Up you go, Lechat."

They climbed the ladder, one behind the other. There were round copper portholes in the cabin, and Maigret saw a woman's face pressed against one for an instant, and then disappear into the semidarkness.

A moment later the hatch opened, and Philippe's head appeared, his hair uncombed, his eyes still puffy with sleep.

"What do you want?" he asked, sullenly.

"A word with Mrs. Wilcox."

"She's not up yet."

"That's not true. I've just seen her."

Philippe was wearing silk pajamas, with blue stripes. There were a few steps to go down in order to enter the cabin, and Maigret, heavy and obstinate, was not waiting to be invited.

"May we come in?"

It was a strange mixture of luxury and disorder, of the refined and the sordid. The deck was meticulously scrubbed and all the brasswork gleamed, the ropes were carefully coiled, the captain's bridge, with its compass and nautical instruments, was as clean as a Dutch kitchen.

Going down the steps, the visitors immediately found themselves in a cabin with mahogany paneling, a table fixed to the floor, two benches with red leather upholstery, but with bottles and glasses lying about on the table, and there were slices of bread, a half-eaten tin of sardines, playing cards; a nauseating smell hung in the air, a mixture of alcohol and beds.

The door of the next cabin, which served as a bedroom, must have been shut in a hurry, and in her flight, Mrs. Wilcox had left a satin slipper upon the floor.

"Please excuse the intrusion," Maigret said politely to Philippe. "You were probably in the middle of breakfast?"

He was looking, without irony, at the half-empty bottles of English beer, a piece of bread which had been bitten into, a scrap of butter in some paper.

"Is this an official search?" questioned the young man, running his fingers through his hair.

"It's whatever you want it to be. Just now, as far as I am concerned, it's a straightforward visit."

"At this hour?"

"Mrs. Wilcox is in the habit of rising late."

The sound of water could be heard on the other side of the door. Philippe would have liked to go away and put on something decent, but that would have meant revealing the too intimate disorder of the second cabin. He had no dressing gown at hand. His pajamas were crumpled. Mechanically he swallowed a mouthful of beer. Lechat had remained on the deck, following the chief inspector's instructions, and must then have been busy with the two sailors.

The latter were not English, as one might have supposed, but came from Nice, probably of Italian origin, to judge by their accents.

"You can sit down, Mr. Pyke," said Maigret, since Philippe omitted to invite them.

Maigret's grandmother always used to go to the first Mass, at six o'clock in the morning, and when everyone else got up they found her in a black silk dress, with a white bonnet on her head, a fire blazing in the hearth, and breakfast served on a starched tablecloth.

Old women had been to the first Mass here, and others would now be making their way diagonally across the square, heading for the open door of the church, with its smell of incense.

As for Mrs. Wilcox, she had already had a drink of beer and in the morning more of the white roots must have been visible in her dyed hair. She went to and fro on the other side of the partition, without being able to be of any assistance to her secretary.

The latter, his cheek slightly swollen where the evening before Polyte had struck him with his fist, looked like a sulky schoolboy in his striped pajamas. For just as there is in every class a fat boy who resembles an India-rubber ball, there is invariably the pupil who spends his free time silently preening himself in his corner while his schoolmates say:

"He's a drip!"

On the walls were hung engravings, but the chief inspector was unable to pronounce on their quality. Some of them were fairly erotic, but without exceeding the limits of good taste.

They looked, Mr. Pyke and himself, rather as though they were in a waiting room, and the Englishman was holding his straw hat between his knees.

Maigret finally lit his pipe.

"How old is your mother, Monsieur de Moricourt?"

"Why do you ask me that?"

"No reason. Judging by your age she must be in her fifties?"

"Forty-five. She had me very young. She married at sixteen."

"Mrs. Wilcox is older than her, isn't she?"

Mr. Pyke lowered his head. Anyone might have thought the chief inspector was doing it deliberately to make everyone feel more uncomfortable. Lechat was more at ease, outside, seated on the rail, chatting with one of the two sailors who was cleaning his nails in the sun.

In the end there was a noise from the door, which opened and Mrs. Wilcox appeared, shutting it again hastily behind her so as not to let the chaos be seen.

She had found time to dress, and make up, but her features, under the thick cosmetics, remained puffed, her eyes anxious.

She must have been pitiable in the morning when she tried to clear her hangover with a bottle of strong beer.

"Grandmother . . . " thought Maigret, in spite of himself.

He rose, greeted her, introduced his companion.

"Perhaps you know Mr. Pyke? He's a fellow country-man of yours, who works at Scotland Yard. He's not here on business. Excuse my disturbing you at such an early hour, Mrs. Wilcox."

She remained, in spite of everything, a lady, and a glance was enough to give Philippe to understand that his attire was indecent.

"Will you excuse me while I go and dress?" he murmured with a nasty look at the chief inspector.

"Perhaps you will feel more at your ease."

"Sit down, gentlemen. Is there anything I can offer you?"

She saw the pipe that Maigret was allowing to go out.

"Do go on smoking. Besides, I'm going to light a cigarette myself."

She forced a smile.

"You must forgive the mess here, but a yacht isn't a house and space is limited."

What was Mr. Pyke thinking at that particular moment? That his French colleague was a brute, or a boor?

Very possibly. Maigret was anyhow not exactly proud of the job he had to do.

"I believe you know Jef de Greef, Mrs. Wilcox?"

"He's a clever young man, and Anna's sweet. They've been on board several times."

"He's said to be a talented painter."

"I believe he is. I've had occasion to buy a canvas from him and I would have been happy to show it to you, only I've sent it off to my villa in Fiesole."

"You've got a villa in Italy?"

"Oh, it's quite a modest little villa. But it's magnificently situated, on a hill, and from the windows you have a view over the whole of Florence. Do you know Florence, inspector?"

"I haven't that pleasure."

"I live there for part of the year. I send everything there that I happen to buy during the course of my wanderings."

She thought she had found firm ground.

"You really don't want anything to drink?"

She was thirsty herself, and eyed the bottle she hadn't had time to finish earlier on, not daring to drink alone.

"Won't you really try some of this beer, which I have sent straight from England?"

He said yes, to please her. She went over to a cupboard which had been turned into an icebox to look for some bottles. Most of the walls of the cabin were actually cupboards, just as the benches concealed chests.

"You've bought a lot of things on your travels, I gather?"

She laughed.

"Who told you that? I buy for the pleasure of buying, it is true. In Istanbul, for example, I always allow myself to be tempted by the salesmen at the bazaar. I come back on board with absolute horrors. At the time, they seem beautiful. Then, when I get back to the villa and find those things . . ."

"Did you meet de Greef in Paris?"

"No. Here only, not so long ago."

"And your secretary?"

"He's been with me for two years now. He's a very cultured boy. We got to know each other at Cannes."

"Was he working?"

"He was reporting for a Paris newspaper."

Moricourt must have had his ear glued to the partition.

"You speak French perfectly, Mrs. Wilcox."

"I was partly educated in Paris. My governess was French."

"Did Marcellin often come on board?"

"Certainly. I think almost everyone on the island has been on board."

"Do you remember the night he died?"

"I think so."

He looked at her hands, which were not trembling.

"He talked a lot about me, that evening."

"That's what I was told. I didn't know who you were. I asked Philippe."

"And did Monsieur de Moricourt know?"

"It appears that you're well known."

"When you left the Arche de Noé . . ."

"Go on."

"Had Marcellin gone already?"

"I couldn't tell you. What I do know is that we went down to the harbor hugging the houses, the mistral was so strong, I was even afraid we shouldn't manage to get back on board."

"Did you set off straightaway in the boat, Monsieur de Moricourt and yourself?"

"Straightaway. What else could we have done? That reminds me that Marcellin came with us as far as the dinghy."

"You didn't meet anyone?"

"There can't have been anybody out at that hour."

"Had de Greef and Anna returned to their boat?"

"Possibly. I can't remember. Wait . . ."

Then Maigret was astounded to hear the precise voice of Mr. Pyke, who, for the first time, was allowing himself to intervene in his investigation. The Yard man said deliberately, yet without appearing to attach too much importance to it:

"At home, Mrs. Wilcox, we should be obliged to remind you that anything you say may be used in evidence against you."

She looked at him, dumbfounded, then looked at Maigret, and there was a sort of panic in her eyes.

"Is this an interrogation?" she asked. "But . . . tell me, chief inspector . . . I presume you don't suspect us, Philippe and me, of having killed this man?"

Maigret was silent for a moment, examining his pipe with deliberation.

"I suspect nobody *a priori*, Mrs. Wilcox. However, this is certainly an interrogation and you have the right not to reply."

"Why shouldn't I reply? We came back straightaway. Even though we shipped water in the dinghy and had to cling to the ladder to climb on board."

"Philippe didn't go out again?"

There was a hesitation in her eyes. The presence of her fellow countryman made her feel uncomfortable.

"We went straight to bed and he couldn't have left the boat without my hearing."

Philippe chose this moment to make his appearance, in white flannels, his hair smoothed down, a freshly lit cigarette at his lips. He wanted to appear bold. He addressed himself directly to Maigret.

"You have some questions to put to me, inspector?"

The latter pretended not to notice him.

"Do you often buy paintings, madame?"

"Fairly often. It's one of my hobbies. Without having exactly what you might call a picture gallery, I have some pretty good ones."

"At Fiesole?"

"At Fiesole, yes."

"Italian masters?"

"I don't rise to that. I'm more modest and content myself with fairly modern works."

"Cézannes or Renoirs, for example?"

"I've a charming little Renoir."

"Degas, Manet, Monet?"

"A Degas drawing, a dancer."

"Van Gogh?"

Maigret was not looking at her, but stared straight at Philippe, who appeared to swallow hard and whose gaze became completely rigid.

"I've just bought a van Gogh."

"How long ago?"

"A few days. What day did we go to Hyères to send it off, Philippe?"

"I don't remember exactly," the latter replied in a colorless voice.

Maigret prompted them.

"Wasn't it the day before or two days before Marcellin's death?"

"Two days before," she said. "I remember it now."

"Did you find the picture here?"

She didn't stop to think, and a moment later she bit her lip.

"It was Philippe," she said, "who through a friend . . ."

She understood, by the silence of the three men, looked at them in turn, then cried:

"What is it, Philippe?"

She had risen with a start, was advancing toward the chief inspector.

"You don't mean? . . . Explain to me! Speak! Why don't you say something? Philippe? What's . . . ?"

The latter still didn't stir.

"Excuse me, madame, but I must take your secretary away."

"Are you arresting him? But I tell you he was here, he didn't leave me all night, that . . ."

She looked at the door of the cabin which served as a bedroom and one could feel that she was on the point of throwing open the door, showing the double bed and shouting:

"How could he have gone without my knowing?"

Maigret and Mr. Pyke had risen as well.

"Will you come with me, Monsieur de Moricourt?"

"Have you a warrant?"

"I shall ask for one from the examining magistrate if you insist, but I don't think that will be the case."

"Are you arresting me?"

"Not yet."

"Where are you taking me?"

"Somewhere where we can have a quiet conversation. Don't you think it would be better that way?"

"Tell me, Philippe . . ." Mrs. Wilcox began.

Without realizing she began to speak to him in English. Philippe wasn't listening to her, or looking at her, or thinking about her anymore. As he climbed onto the deck, she was not even given a look of farewell.

"This won't get you very far," he said to Maigret.

"That's very possible."

"Perhaps you're going to handcuff me?"

It was still Sunday and the *Cormorant*, moored to the jetty, was disgorging its passengers in their bright-colored clothes. Already some tourists, perched on rocks, were busy fishing.

Mr. Pyke left the cabin last, and when he took his place in the dinghy, he was very red. Lechat, surprised to see another passenger, didn't know what to say.

Maigret, seated at the stern, allowed his left hand to trail in the water, as he used to do when he was small and his father took him in a boat on the pond.

The bells were still sending their circles of sound into the air.

9

They stopped outside the grocer's to ask the mayor for the key. He was busy serving customers and he shouted something to his wife, who was small and pale, with a bun at the nape of her neck. She searched for a long while. During all this time Philippe remained waiting, between Maigret and Mr. Pyke, his face set obstinately in a sulky expression, and it resembled more than ever a school scene, with the punished schoolboy and the heavy, implacable headmaster.

One would never have believed that so many people could have come off the *Cormorant*. True, other boats had made the crossing that morning. Until the trippers had had time to stream off to the beaches, the square looked like an invasion.

Anna could be seen, in the semiobscurity of the cooperative, with her net bag, wearing her sunsuit, while de Greef was sitting with Charlot on the terrace of the Arche.

These two had seen Philippe passing by between the detectives. They had followed them with their eyes. They were free themselves, with a table in front of them and a bottle of cool wine on the table.

Maigret had said a few words in an undertone to Lechat who had stayed behind.

The mayor's wife finally brought the key and a few minutes later Maigret was pushing open the door of the town hall, and immediately opened the window on account of the dust and mustiness.

"Sit down, Moricourt."

"Is that an order?"

"Precisely."

He pushed over to him one of the folding chairs used for the July 14 celebrations. Mr. Pyke appeared to have understood that on these occasions the chief inspector didn't like to see people standing, for he unfolded a chair in his turn and settled himself in a corner.

"I suppose you have nothing to say to me?"

"Am I under arrest?"

"Yes."

"I didn't kill Marcellin."

"What else?"

"Nothing. I shall say nothing more. You can question me to your heart's content and use all the vile methods you have at your command to make people speak, but I'll still say nothing."

How like a vicious child! Perhaps because of the impressions of that morning, Maigret couldn't manage to take him seriously, to get it into his head that he was dealing with a man.

The chief inspector didn't sit down. He walked up and down aimlessly, touching a rolled-up flag or the bust of the Republic, stood for a moment in front of the window, and saw some little girls in white crossing the square in the care of two nuns with winged bonnets. He hadn't been so far out just now in being reminded of a first communion.

The islanders were wearing clean trousers that morning, made of cloth, of a blue that became deep and rich in the sunlight of the square, and the white of their shirts was dazzling. A game of boules was already starting. Monsieur Émile was making for the post office with his careful tread.

"I suppose you realize you're a little rat?"

Maigret, enormous beside Philippe, looked him up and down, and the young man instinctively raised his hands to protect his face.

"I said a little rat, a rat who's afraid, who's a coward. There are people who break into flats and take risks. Others only go for old ladies, pinch rare books from them to resell them, and when they are caught, start crying, begging forgiveness and talking about their poor mothers."

Mr. Pyke appeared to be making himself as small and as motionless as possible so as in no way to obstruct his colleague. One couldn't even hear him breathing, but the sounds from the island came in through the open window and mingled oddly with the chief inspector's voice.

"Who first got the idea of the forged paintings?"

"I shall only reply in the presence of a lawyer."

"So that your unfortunate mother will have to bleed herself white to pay for a well-known barrister for you! You'll have to have a well-known one, won't you? You're a repugnant creature, Moricourt!"

He stalked up and down, with his hands behind his back, more like a headmaster than ever.

"At my school we had a boy who was rather like you. Like you he was a drip. From time to time he needed a beating up, and when we gave him one, our teacher took care to turn his back or else to leave the playground. You had one yesterday evening and you didn't budge, you stayed there, pale and trembling in your place, beside the old woman who keeps you alive. It was I who asked Polyte to give you a hiding because I wanted to know your reactions, because I wasn't yet sure."

"Are you intending to hit me again?"

He was trying to sneer, but one could tell that he was transfixed with fear.

"There are various species of rat, Moricourt, and unfortunately there are some that one somehow never manages to send to prison. I tell you straightaway that I shall do all in my power to get you there."

Ten times he turned back toward the young man in his chair, and each time the latter made an instinctive gesture to protect his face.

"Admit that the idea of the pictures was yours. You'll end by confessing, even if I have to spend three days and three nights at it. I've met a tougher nut than you. He sneered too, when he arrived at the Quai des Orfèvres. He was well dressed like you. It was a long business. There were five or six of us taking it in turns. After thirty-six hours do you know what happened to him? Do you know how we discovered that he was giving in at last? By the smell! A smell as foul as himself! He had just relieved himself in his trousers."

He looked at Moricourt's beautiful white trousers, then ordered him point-blank:

"Take off your tie."

"Why?"

"Do you want me to do it myself? Good! Now, undo your shoes. Remove the laces. You'll see, in a few hours you'll begin to look a bit more guilty."

"You haven't the right . . ."

"I'll take it! You wondered how to squeeze more money from the mad old woman you had attached yourself to. Your lawyer will probably plead that it's immoral to allow fortunes to remain in the hands of women like her and will claim that it's an irresistible temptation. That doesn't concern us for the moment. All that's a matter for the jury. Because she bought pictures and didn't know anything about them you told yourself that there was big money to be made, and you got together with de Greef. I wonder whether it wasn't you that made him come to Porquerolles."

"De Greef is a little saint, isn't he?"

"Another kind of rat. How many forgeries did he make for your old woman?"

"I've told you I shall say nothing."

"The van Gogh can't have been the first. Only it happens that somebody spotted that particular one, probably when it wasn't quite finished. Marcellin used to wander around almost anywhere. He used to climb on board de Greef's yacht as well as the *North Star*. I suppose he caught the Dutchman in the middle of signing a canvas with a name that wasn't his own. Then he saw the same canvas in Mrs. Wilcox's possession and he tumbled to it. It took him a bit of time to find out how the system was worked. He wasn't sure. He had never even heard of van Gogh and he telephoned a girlfriend to find out about him."

Philippe was staring fixedly at the floor, a peevish look on his face.

"I don't say it was you who killed him."

"I didn't kill him."

"You're probably too much of a coward for that sort of a job. Marcellin told himself that as the two of you were getting fat off the old woman's bank balance there was no reason why he shouldn't be a third. He put it to you. You wouldn't play. Then, to dot all the i's, he began to talk about his friend Maigret. How much did Marcellin ask?"

"I shan't answer."

"I've plenty of time. That night, Marcellin was killed."

"I have an alibi."

"Namely that at the time of his death you were in the grandmother's bed."

One could smell, even from the small town-hall room, the apéritifs that were being served on the terrace at the Arche. De Greef must still be there. Probably Anna had joined him with her provisions. Lechat, at a neighboring table, was watching him, and if necessary would stop him going away.

As for Charlot, he had surely realized by now that, at all events, he was too late. He was another who had been hoping to have his cut!

"Are you intending to talk, Philippe?"

"No."

"Note that I'm not trying to make you do so by telling stories. I'm not telling you that we've got proof, that de Greef has taken the bait. You'll talk in the end, because you're a coward, because you're poisonous. Give me your cigarettes."

Maigret took the packet the young man handed to him and threw it out of the window.

"May I ask you to do me a service, Mr. Pyke? Will you go and ask Lechat, who is on the terrace at the Arche, to bring in the Dutchman? Without the girl. I'd also like Jojo to bring us a few bottles of beer."

As though from scruple, he did not utter a word during his colleague's absence. He went on walking up and down, his hands behind his back, and the Sunday life continued on the other side of the window.

"Come in, de Greef. If you had a tie, I should tell you to take it off, and the same with your shoelaces."

"Am I under arrest?"

Maigret contented himself with a nod.

"Sit down. Not too near your friend Philippe. Give me your cigarettes and throw away the one you've got stuck in your mouth."

"Have you a warrant?"

"I'm going to send for one by telegraph, in your two names, so there'll be no more doubt on the subject."

He sat down in the place the mayor must have occupied for marriages.

"One of you two killed Marcellin. To tell the truth it doesn't much matter which, since you're each as guilty as the other."

Jojo came in, with a tray covered with bottles and glasses, then stood nonplussed in front of the two young men.

"Don't be afraid, Jojo. They're just two dirty little killers. Don't start talking about it outside immediately or we'll have the whole population at the window and the Sunday trippers into the bargain."

Maigret was taking his time, looking at the two young men in turn. The Dutchman was much the calmer and there was no trace of bravado about him.

"Perhaps I'd do better to leave you to settle it between the two of you? When all's said and done, it concerns one of you. There is in fact one person who will probably have his head lopped off or else will spend the rest of his days in a penal settlement, while the other will get away with a few years in prison. Which?"

Already the "drip" was shifting in his chair and one might have thought he was going to put up his hand, as if at school.

"Unfortunately the law cannot take into account true responsibility. For my part I would happily put the two of you in the same bag, with this difference, however, that I should have a tiny scrap of sympathy for de Greef."

Philippe was still shifting, ill at ease, visibly discontented.

"Admit, de Greef, that you didn't do it just for the money? You don't want to answer, either? As you wish. I bet that you've been amusing yourself painting forgeries for quite some time, just to prove you're no spare-time painter, no mere dauber. Have you sold a lot?

"Never mind! What a revenge on the people who don't understand you if you had one of your works, signed with a famous name, hanging in line at the Louvre, or an Amsterdam museum!

"We shall be seeing your latest works. We'll have them sent from Fiesole. At the trial the experts will argue over them. You're going to live through some great moments, de Greef!"

It was almost amusing to see Philippe's expression, at once disgusted and angry, during this little speech. The two of them looked more and more like schoolboys. Philippe was jealous of the words Maigret was addressing to his classmate and had to hold himself in so as not to protest.

"Admit, Monsieur de Greef, that you aren't really annoyed that it hasn't come off!"

Even down to the "Monsieur," which wounded Moricourt to his very soul.

"When no one else knows but yourself, it's not much fun in the end. You don't love your life, Monsieur de Greef."

"Nor yours, nor the one people wanted me to lead."

"You don't love anything."

"I don't love myself."

"Nor do you love that little girl whom you only carried off out of defiance, to infuriate her parents. Since when have you been wanting to kill one of your fellow creatures? I don't say from necessity, to gain money or to suppress an embarrassing witness. I'm speaking of killing for the sake of killing, to see what it's like, what reactions one has. And even to hit the body afterwards with a hammer to prove that one has strong nerves."

A thin smile twisted the Dutchman's lips, and Philippe was furtively watching him, without understanding.

"Would you like me to predict now what's going to happen? You've decided, both of you, to keep silent. You are convinced that there is no proof against you. There was no witness of Marcellin's death. Nobody on the island heard the shot, because of the mistral. The weapon hasn't been found; probably it's safe at the bottom of the sea. I haven't taken the trouble to make a search. Fingerprints won't tell us anything more. It will be a long inquiry. The magistrate will question you patiently, will find out about your antecedents, and the newspapers will talk a lot about you. They won't fail to splash the fact that you are both of good family.

"Your Montparnasse friends, de Greef, will emphasize that you are talented. You will be represented as a fantastic, misunderstood being.

"People will also talk about the two slim volumes of verse which Moricourt has had published."

It may be imagined how delighted the latter was to see a good point awarded him at last!

"The reporters will go and interview the judge at Groningen, and Madame de Moricourt at Saumur. The gutter press will laugh at Mrs. Wilcox and no doubt her embassy will make representations for her name to be mentioned as seldom as possible."

He drank half a glass of beer at a gulp and went and sat on the window sill, his back turned to the sunny square.

"De Greef will remain silent, because it's in his temperament, because he's not afraid."

"And I'll talk?" sneered Philippe.

"You'll talk. Because you're a drip through and through, because in the eyes of the world, you'll be the nasty piece of work, because you'll try to worm your way out of it, because you're a coward and you'll convince yourself that by talking you'll save your precious skin."

De Greef turned to his companion, an indefinable smile on his lips.

"You'll talk, tomorrow probably, when you find several hefty chaps, in a real police station, questioning you with their fists. You don't like being hit, Phillippe."

"They haven't the right."

"Nor have you the right to swindle a poor woman who no longer knows what she's doing."

"Or who knows only too well! It's because she's got money that you go to her defense."

Maigret didn't even have to advance toward him for him to lift up his hands again.

"You'll talk all the more when you see that de Greef has a better chance of getting off than you have."

"He was on the island."

"He had an alibi, as well. If you were with the old woman, he was with Anna . . ."

"Anna will say . . ."

"Will say what?"

"Nothing."

Lunch had begun at the Arche. Jojo cannot have remained altogether silent, or else people could smell something in the air, for silhouettes could be seen from time to time roving round the town hall.

Presently there would be a whole crowd.

"I've a good mind to leave the two of you alone. What do you think, Mr. Pyke? With someone to watch them, of course, or otherwise we'd risk finding them in small pieces. Will you stay, Lechat?"

The latter went and settled himself, his elbows on the table, and, for want of an apéritif or a white wine, poured himself a glass of beer.

Maigret and his British colleague found themselves outside once more in the sun, which was at its hottest, and strolled a few yards in silence.

"Are you disappointed, Mr. Pyke?" asked the chief inspector finally, watching him from the corner of his eye.

"Why?"

"I don't know. You came to France to find out our methods and you discover there are none. Moricourt will talk. I could have made him talk straightaway."

"By employing the method you spoke of?"

"That one or another. Whether he talks or not, it's of no real importance. He'll retract. He'll confess again, then retract again. You'll see doubt being insinuated into the minds of the jury. The two lawyers will argue like cat and dog, each whitening his own client, each placing the entire responsibility on his colleague's client."

They didn't need to raise themselves on tiptoe to see the two young men, through the town-hall window, sitting on their chairs. On the terrace of the Arche, Charlot was eating his lunch, with his girlfriend on his right, and on his left Ginette, who seemed to be explaining from afar to the chief inspector that she hadn't been able to refuse the invitation.

"It's more pleasant to deal with professionals."

Perhaps he was thinking of Charlot.

"But those are seldom the ones who kill. Real crimes occur partly by accident. These lads started by playing, without attempting to find out where it was leading them. It was almost like a good joke. To unload pictures signed with famous names on a dotty old woman, worth thousands! And then one fine morning some odd character called Marcellin climbs onto the deck of the boat at an inopportune moment . . . ."

"Do you feel sorry for them?"

Maigret shrugged, without replying.

"You'll see how the psychiatrists will discuss their respective degrees of responsibility."

Mr. Pyke, screwing up his eyes on account of the sun, gazed at length at his colleague, as though he were trying to plumb his thoughts, then said simply:

"Ah!"

The chief inspector didn't ask whether he had just arrived at a conclusion. He spoke of something else, asking:

"Do you like the Mediterranean, Mr. Pyke?"

And as Mr. Pyke, hesitating, was preparing his answer, he went on:

"I wonder whether the air isn't too strong for me. We shall probably be able to get off this evening."

The white church tower had become set against the sky, at once hard and transparent. The mayor, intrigued, was looking in from outside through the window of his hall. What was Charlot doing? He could be seen rising from his table and setting off hurriedly for the harbor.

Maigret watched him for a moment, frowning, then grunted:

"As long as . . ."

He rushed off in the same direction, followed by Mr. Pyke, who didn't understand.

When they arrived within sight of the jetty, Charlot was already on the deck of the small yacht, ironically christened:

Flower of Love.

He paused for a moment, leaning on the rail, examining the interior, disappeared, then returned to the deck carrying someone in his arms.

When the two men arrived in their turn, Anna was stretched out on the deck, and Charlot, without any shame, took off her sunsuit, laying bare in the sun a full and heavy bosom.

"Didn't it occur to you?" he said, bitterly.

"Veronal?"

"There's an empty tube on the cabin floor."

There were five, then ten, then a whole crowd round the body of Mademoiselle Bebelmans. The island doctor came up slowly, and said in a broken voice:

"I've brought an emetic, in case there's a chance."

Mrs. Wilcox was on the deck of her yacht, accompanied by one of her sailors, and they were handing a pair of binoculars to one another.

"So you see, Mr. Pyke, I make mistakes as well. She realized that de Greef had nothing to fear except her evidence and she was afraid of talking."

He pushed through the crowd that had gathered in front of the town hall. Lechat had closed the window. The two young men were still in their places, the bottles of beer on the table.

Maigret started to prowl up and down the room like a bear, stopped in front of Philippe de Moricourt, and, suddenly, without any warning whatever, this time without the young man having time to protect himself, he struck him full in the face with his hand.

It relieved him. In an almost calm voice, he murmured:

"I beg your pardon, Mr. Pyke."

Then to de Greef, who was watching him and trying to understand:

"Anna is dead."

He didn't bother to question them that day. He tried not to see the coffin which was still in its corner, the famous coffin of old Benoît, which had already been used for Marcellin and which was to be used for the young girl from Ostend.

Ironically, Benoît's hirsute head, well in evidence, was distinguishable among the crowd.

Lechat and the two men, handcuffed by their wrists, set off for Giens Point in a fishing boat.

Maigret and Mr. Pyke took the *Cormorant* at five o'clock, and Ginette was there, likewise Charlot and his dancing girl, and all the trippers who had spent the day on the beaches of the island.

The *North Star* was riding at anchor at the harbor entrance. Maigret, scowling, was smoking his pipe and as his lips moved, Mr. Pyke leaned toward him to ask:

"I beg your pardon? You were saying?"

"I said: dirty wretches!"

With which he quickly turned away his head and gazed into the depths of the water.